"SAMI, DON'T BE AFRAID OF ME," DILLON SAID.

She looked at him then—a mistake. His eyes held her. How could she explain that the feelings he evoked in her terrified her? That she'd never, ever felt this strange, delicious, and fuzzy feeling before? That he knocked her for such a loop, she'd never find her way out?

"I—I'm not."

"I wish it were different," he said quietly.

Despite the wonderfully cool breeze that gently ruffled her hair, she felt warm. Too warm. Suddenly he was so close their legs touched.

He brought his mouth to hers lightly. "I wanted to talk to you here, really talk to you."

"Talk?" She could hardly think.

"But every time I get this close, I feel like doing something else."

"Dillon—"

The rest of her words were lost as his lips grazed hers once, then again, before tracing a trail to her ear. He tugged on the sensitive lobe with his teeth, and a little sound escaped from her. He pulled back and their gazes locked. She struggled with control, but lost the fight when he pulled her close against him. . . .

WHAT ARE *LOVESWEPT* ROMANCES?

They are stories of true romance and touching emotion. We believe those two very important ingredients are constants in our highly sensual and very believable stories in the LOVE-SWEPT line. Our goal is to give you, the reader, stories of consistently high quality that may sometimes make you laugh, sometimes make you cry, but are always fresh and creative and contain many delightful surprises within their pages.

Most romance fans read an enormous number of books. Those they truly love, they keep. Others may be traded with friends and soon forgotten. We hope that each LOVESWEPT romance will be a treasure—a "keeper." We will always try to publish

LOVE STORIES YOU'LL NEVER FORGET BY AUTHORS YOU'LL ALWAYS REMEMBER

The Editors

CHARMED
AND
DANGEROUS

JILL
SHALVIS

BANTAM BOOKS
NEW YORK · TORONTO · LONDON · SYDNEY · AUCKLAND

CHARMED AND DANGEROUS

A Bantam Book / May 1997

ISBN 0-553-44601-0

Published simultaneously in the United States and Canada

*Bantam Books are published by Bantam Books, a division of Bantam
Doubleday Dell Publishing Group, Inc. Its trademark, consisting of the
words "Bantam Books" and the portrayal of a rooster, is Registered in
U.S. Patent and Trademark Office and in other countries. Marca Regis-
trada. Bantam Books, 1540 Broadway, New York, New York 10036.*

PRINTED IN THE UNITED STATES OF AMERICA

OPM   10 9 8 7 6 5 4 3 2 1

To my three little angels, who always let me work when I needed to, and who hardly ever smeared the keyboard with chocolate.

PROLOGUE

It felt good to be back in the States. Dillon Kinley worked the controls of the Cessna 350 as he prepared for landing. He couldn't see the lush green Los Angeles forest through the thick cloud cover, but he knew it was there. Yep, it felt good to be back on his home turf—where people respected freedom and one could drink the water without taking a pill.

The storm battered his poor plane. The rain pummeled his windshield. Dillon smiled grimly and landed with the ease of a survivalist who knew how to fly any aircraft ever built. After the conditions he'd flown in over the past few years, he knew he could have landed backward with his eyes closed.

He sat for a minute and took it all in. He'd spent only five years in the Middle East, though it felt like fifty. He'd worked long and hard for the U.S. government, but now he had plans, the first of which was to rent a car.

Dillon let himself in to the San Fernando Valley house he'd grown up in, assaulted by bittersweet memories. They'd been a tight unit, Dillon and his family. Generous love and complete loyalty without fail. He missed those days, but they were over for good. Had been ever since six years before, when his parents had been killed in a plane crash. The house was empty, as it would be for the rest of its days.

On the mantel were pictures, precious little moments frozen in time. He picked up one of his father holding his mother close, whispering a secret in her ear. He could see his mother's eyes, alight with love and sparkling with mischief. Dillon ran a finger over the dusty glass and sighed. At the next picture, a reluctant smile came to his face, easing his heart. Two laughing teenagers grinned at him, arms slung around each other's necks, holding basketballs. His brother, Kevin, wore a lopsided smile that had a lump sticking in Dillon's throat.

He missed his brother.

Kevin, like his parents, was gone. Ironically, he, too, had died in a plane wreck—but his hadn't been an accident. Eight months earlier, Dillon had gotten a frantic letter from his brother saying he'd gotten himself a job as an airplane mechanic in a small, private airport called Reed Aviation. Apparently Kevin, never a stranger to trouble, had gotten himself knee-deep in it this time, and he'd wanted Dillon to come help him. His letter said he'd witnessed something he shouldn't have. Dillon, used to such letters, arranged for a leave, which had been denied. Two months later his brother was dead, leaving Dillon to try to deal with the stabbing guilt for not taking his brother more seriously.

Now, six months later, Dillon had finally gotten his leave—and he had a score to settle.

ONE

The phone rang, and from her position in the large, empty maintenance hangar, Sami Reed sighed. She headed directly into the pouring rain, sprinting the fifty-foot dash to the lobby door. By the time she yanked it open, she was drenched.

She ran to the front desk, leaning for the phone. "Please, please," she whispered, "be the fuel rep canceling our meeting."

Snapping the receiver up on the seventh ring, she kept her weight stretched over the desk, gasping for breath. "Reed Aviation," she just managed, dripping water everywhere. The dial tone annoyed her into verbalizing very unladylike thoughts.

"I agree," said a deep, amused voice. "Besides, with a gait like that you should be doing more than answering phones."

Sami jumped down and whirled at the words, blushing when she saw the tall figure standing at the lobby's front door. The entire wall to the airstrip was glass, and she knew he'd had a perfect view of her long, graceless run from the hangar.

He stomped his shoes on the mat to rid them of the mud and water he'd accumulated in the flooded parking lot, then flung back his hood. Water flew as he raised his head, resting his startling sea-green gaze on Sami.

She couldn't speak. Funny, she thought vaguely, that had never happened to her before. Men didn't affect her that way. No one did.

"I have a meeting with Sam Reed," he said in a low, gravelly voice, seeming incredibly tall and imposing standing there framed in the doorway.

"Yes, of course." She smiled politely, but she knew the smile must have appeared stiff. Why did the fuel company have to be so prompt? "Come back to my office. You're early."

"Early." He grimaced as he followed her through the lobby and down a hall into the last office. "I'm nearly two hours late. That narrow two-lane road into this town is pathetic."

How well she knew. Any other day, with any other person, Sami would have agreed, joking about her latest ticket. But today she had nothing to laugh about. Instead, she had to concentrate on getting this fuel representative to agree to give Reed Aviation fuel, and not charge them until she sold it. It was the only way to get the business back on its feet. She sat at her desk.

"I'd like to see the space I've rented and sign the contract," the man said, still standing.

Sami stared at him in confusion. Officially, Reed Aviation was closed to business—but only temporarily. As acting president for her ailing father, she intended to get the fixed operating base open again by the following week. They'd closed several months earlier because of the tragic accident that had caused the death of an employee and the loss of their biggest client's prized jet. They'd lost the client, but that didn't hurt at all compared to the loss of a cherished friend and brilliant mechanic.

Unfortunately for Sami, she had more important things to worry about, such as how she was going to open again as she'd promised her father. But Sami had confidence in her start-up consultant abilities and knew she could handle it. What she was having a hard time handling was this man's intriguing eyes as they settled on her. She felt as though he was waiting . . . but for what she couldn't imagine.

"The contract," he repeated impatiently. "I'd like to sign it."

"The contract," she said inanely, standing slowly. How could eyes so light look so intensely deep? "You're not from American Petroleum?"

"No. Where's Sam Reed?"

"I'm *Sami* Reed," she said, hoping to enjoy his start of surprise, but he didn't so much as blink.

His gaze ran down her length, all the way to the floor where her dripping hair had left puddles, then slowly back up again. Unbelievably, her breath caught.

"I'm Dillon Kinley," he said in that slow, deep voice. "Where's the space I'm renting?"

Her new client. Her smile defrosted. A reprieve from the petroleum representative! Sami couldn't have been more relieved to see him. She knew better than anyone had badly they needed Kinley's charter business. They needed business period. As a small airport far from nowhere, they depended mostly on wealthy clients flying in and out of their second homes at whim. "I've never heard your name before, and I'm familiar with most of the charters around here," she said conversationally as she turned from him to gather his contract from its file.

"I'm new to the area."

"Where did you come from?" she asked curiously.

"Do you play twenty questions with all your clients, Ms. Reed?"

She looked at him, startled by his sudden briskness. "Do you object to being friendly, Mr. Kinley?"

He stood absolutely still, and she could see how carefully he held his tall, rangy body, almost as if he were prepared at all times for trouble. "No. Not if that's all it is."

She handed him the contract, wondering at this man who looked at her as if she had a hidden agenda. "I'm not drilling you. Your business doesn't interest me, except of course, whether you can pay your rent."

He didn't crack a smile, just lowered his gaze to study the contract. He had deep squint lines, she noticed, probably from too many times in the cockpit without sunglasses. His sun-streaked blond hair still clung damply to his head. He had shrugged out of his coat, leaving tailor-made charcoal trousers with a soft-looking, forest-green chambray shirt rolled to the elbows, revealing well-tanned arms, hard and corded with strength. He was, in short, the most gorgeous man she'd ever spoken to.

He lifted his gaze and caught her staring. She cleared her throat and studied the ceiling, mortified. She'd never stared like that, never.

"Where's the owner, Howard Reed?" he asked.

"He's taken a leave of absence."

"You're related?"

"He's my father. Are the terms of the contract as you expected?" She hoped, oh, how she hoped.

"Yes."

She let out a slow sigh of relief, then promptly sucked it in again when she looked at him. His catlike eyes still scrutinized her closely. She spoke to hide her unease around him. "You understand you've agreed to use our airport as your charter's base. You've rented an office and half of hangar one," she began, uncomfortably aware of him. "You can house two planes there nightly, no more. More than two incoming flights a day and you'll be charged for landing services as well. Also, you're responsible for your own insurance coverage for the charter business since the airport is strictly your landlord."

She made the mistake of looking at him.

Dillon Kinley *could* smile after all, and it was something to see. "I can read."

Sami reeled, hoping to God he didn't smile often. It could be embarrassing to be rendered speechless during a business meeting. "I like to go over details verbally," she managed to say without stuttering. "It could save trouble later."

"Do you anticipate trouble?"

The only trouble she anticipated would come from his flashing that lethal weapon he called a smile. If this was what lust felt like, she'd just as soon have heartburn. "No." She sat and crossed her legs.

His eyes flashed heat. "You manage this whole place?"

She reminded herself she needed his business. Desperately needed it. "I do my best. You do realize that the services offered don't start until the first of next week. That's when my employees will be back and we reopen for business."

"Why did you close?"

"My father became ill."

His eyes narrowed, and Sami would have sworn her answer disappointed him. But it was the truth—or part of it. Six months, and it still hurt to discuss Kevin's death.

She jumped up. "I'll show you to your office." She scooted past Dillon, giving him a wide berth. Still, their shoulders brushed and she felt it to her toes. He didn't so much as blink, but she knew the connection had jarred him too. What was it about him that made her feel so . . . aware? They walked back through the lobby, silent.

"This place looks pretty fancy for a small, private airport," he commented.

As much as Sami loved her father, she felt the same way. They were only an airport. Private planes flew in and out. Pilots bought fuel. They paid for maintenance and to be housed overnight if necessary. Nothing fancy. So why had he put the company in financial jeopardy by spending capital decorating the lobby to resemble an expensive office interior instead of updating his antiquated equipment? If he'd been more careful, she wouldn't now have to hire out space. "Glad you like it."

"I didn't say I did."

She held her temper—barely. "I see."

"Don't get me wrong," he said evenly, though his eyes laughed at her, telling her he knew exactly what it cost her to remain polite. "I like luxury plenty. But a private airport should be drafty, noisy, smell like petroleum, and feel like home."

How could she argue something she believed with all her heart? She opened the hangar. She loved this place, and knew that here, Dillon would find home. The hangar stretched out before them, half the size of a football field. With the wide north and south doors open, the stormy afternoon light poured through. So did the wind.

She inhaled deeply and noticed Dillon did the same. Huge, drafty, and yes, the smell of fuel filled the air. Nothing like home, she thought, hugging her arms around herself, wishing she'd stopped for a coat. A large gale of wind blasted through with a tunnel effect, whipping Sami's wide skirt up, exposing a vast expanse of leg. Awkwardly, she shoved at it, but not before she caught Dillon's interested gaze lingering downward.

"I imagine a dress isn't the easiest thing to be wearing out here," he ventured evenly.

It would do her no good at all to rise to the bait and tell him she'd worn the dress hoping to impress the fuel man. "You wouldn't know the half of it," she muttered, and he flashed a roguish grin that raised her blood pressure uncomfortably. She might have stopped to admire that smile, but she did heartily dislike being laughed at—and she had the uneasy feeling he knew it. She doubted Dillon Kinley missed much.

"I'll have keys made for you." She spoke loudly to be heard over the wind. "What day next week will you be back?"

"Tomorrow."

The finality to his voice didn't disturb her as much

as the sudden cold glint of his eyes. "But I won't have staff until—"

"—I know, you've said. I'll handle my own phone and correspondence until you reopen." He walked away from her a few feet, surveying the hangar. Something about the way he held himself spoke of his ability to handle anything. He stood there, his feet firmly planted a large step apart, his hands on his hips, looking like the owner of the place, rather than the tenant.

"There's no line crew to help you land."

"I'm used to much rougher conditions than this, believe me."

Somehow, the thought of being alone with this tough-looking, sarcastic, intelligent, and annoying man didn't appeal to her. "I can't even guarantee you fuel," she protested with one last-ditch effort. "I'm arranging to lease the fuel trucks, but until then you'd be at the mercy of ours, and they don't always work. At the moment, we're just a shell of an airport."

He slid his hands into his pockets and lifted a brow. "There's always Mountain Aircraft at the other end of the runway."

Their competitor. Okay, so he knew far more about her than she knew of him. She'd have to remedy that. But if he wanted to rough it, fine. She'd get one more week of income out of him.

As for Dillon, he couldn't care less about the extra money he'd owe Sami Reed. He wanted answers about Kevin and he wanted them yesterday.

He didn't think Sami would tell him a thing. Nope, Ms. Reed was a cool one, with her icy looks and distant demeanor. Oh, she had beauty. Straight amber hair that fell to her shoulders, matching whiskey-colored

eyes that made him think of a warm winter night, and a
long, lithe body to die for. But it had been Reed running the place six months ago when Kevin had died,
not Sami. He glanced at the woman next to him and
found her lost in thought, staring out at the quickly
vanishing clouds.

"Isn't it beautiful?" she asked, her voice a little
dreamy.

"Yeah." He loved it, actually, but was surprised she
felt the same.

"I've loved this place since I was a child," she murmured, still looking out of the huge, open doors. "I
never tire of it."

Since she was a child? Dillon's ears perked up. Ms.
Reed just might be more help than he realized. "You
spent a lot of time here?"

"No," she said flatly, leaving him to wonder at the
brief flash of sadness he'd seen in her expression. She'd
shrugged off her reverie. "Your office is this way."

He had two sets of windows, one opened to the
runway, the other opened into the hangar. From his
desk chair he could see all the way across the hangar
and into the far left window of Sami's office. He could
see her chair. He thought of her luscious long legs and
grinned, for the first time in weeks feeling almost
cheerful.

"Not a bad view," he said.

Her eyes narrowed, and he suspected good manners
alone kept her from commenting. "Then you'll sign?"
She held out a pen.

She didn't like him very much, and that thought
made his grin wider. On that score, they were very
even. His reasons for being there didn't remotely

match what she believed. But he wasn't leaving until he discovered the truth.

Sami picked up the contract, and with great grace she left his office, walking across the long, echoing hangar. Dillon watched her, listening to the almost musical sound of her heels, until she disappeared.

Sami muttered to herself as she opened the mail. Bills, bills, and more bills. Absently, she read the plain piece of white paper with its computer-typed words, then read it again in disbelief.

Kevin's death was not an accident.

With hands that shook, Sami smoothed out the paper. The tragic accident that had killed Kevin, her favorite mechanic, was never far from her mind. But why this letter now, six months later? She searched the trash for the envelope. Postmark—Bear Pass. No return address.

Thinking it just a sick joke, she stuffed the letter in her purse and drooped in her chair. Her frustrations grew daily, starting with the constant battle with the petroleum people to provide her fuel for her clients that flew in and out, and ending with her ongoing struggle to keep her father happy. Now this letter.

Like most things about Reed Aviation, Sami hadn't known Kevin all that well. She'd only met him the few times she'd managed to convince her father to let her visit the airport from her home on the East Coast. But she'd found in Kevin one of those rare and treasured instant friendships. She missed him.

Her phone rang, and she picked it up. "Samantha,"

a gruff voice boomed out. "Tell me what's happening there."

Her father still lay in his hospital bed, recovering from the latest in a series of heart attacks that had plagued him over the past six months. He had strict orders from his physician not to so much as think of an airplane, but he wanted to know the latest financial information. "You're not supposed to be working."

"It's hard to be idle, Sami."

"I know," she said gently. After spending her entire life without her father due to a messy, bitter divorce, she was right where she wanted to be. And if she had any lingering resentment that he hadn't made more of an effort to be a real father to her over the years, she'd squelch it.

"What's this I hear about running a charter?"

She should have known she couldn't keep it from him. "I've rented space to Kinley Charters."

After a heavy silence, he said, "You need licenses from—"

"—Got them."

"You need approval for—"

"—Got it." She shifted files around her scarred mahogany desk and fiddled with her pencil. She could practically hear her father's blood pressure rise. "Please, don't worry."

"I'm not." He sighed heavily. "I really wanted to run my own charter."

Her heart twisted. "We don't have the resources to make that kind of commitment, and we need the funds from this tenant."

"Humph."

"You spent a lot of money on the lobby," she said carefully. "Not so much on our equipment."

"So?"

"It just seems . . . extravagant."

"It's still my business," he said stiffly.

She'd never crossed him before, had never had the chance. The thought made her nervous. She did it anyway. "But it doesn't make sense—" She stopped abruptly at the ominous blip of his heart monitor, then eased him gently off the phone. She didn't have the heart to tell him Reed Aviation still hovered just above bankruptcy, and she'd have to use all her resources and every spare moment she had just to keep them afloat.

Which made it all the more annoying when she wasted the next five full minutes staring out the window at her new client, as he marked the spots his planes would be tied down at. Once, he straightened those broad shoulders and looked in her direction, those sharp eyes searching her out. Like a silly schoolgirl, she'd ducked.

She was losing it, she decided. Definitely losing it.

Flying domestic would be like a paid vacation, Dillon thought. He couldn't have picked a better place. Bear Pass was a mountain resort. A perfect place to target customers who wanted to commute the one hundred miles to Los Angeles to work.

He had some well-laid plans to put to the test. Howard Reed had harbored a ruthless reputation. He'd catered to a wealthy sort of clientele and treated his employees badly. But that had been before he'd fallen ill and supposedly begged the daughter he'd ignored all her life to drop everything and run the show for him while he recovered.

Dillon had to admit, he'd been thrown by the fact Reed no longer ran the place. His very female, beautiful, businesslike daughter did. One whose fathomless eyes hinted at deep secrets, but whether those were personal or business, he had yet to find out. He fervently hoped to use whatever they were to help him solve the mystery of his brother's death.

He certainly wasn't used to being at odd ends with a female. Not one who looked like she did. But now, thinking of her soft, bemused expression when she'd watched the sky, he couldn't picture her using her father's harsh techniques. He could be very wrong, but he'd grown accustomed to following his instincts. They'd saved his life more than once, and they'd yet to fail him.

He had to smile as he remembered her running like a demon in heels across the runway in the rain to catch the phone. She'd thrown herself over the desk, completely oblivious to the way her terrific legs dangled over the counter, how her dress had swung provocatively high up on her thighs. No, that wasn't a picture he'd soon forget.

Neither was her obvious relief when he'd shown up to sign the contract. If only she knew how he'd counted on her being so desperate. His smile faded slightly. He'd purposely provoked her in his office. That bothered him. Since when did he get off on being rude to a woman?

He shook his head. There was just something about her . . . and it disturbed him more than he wanted to admit that she might have had a hand in his brother's death.

Abruptly, he left his office and headed across the hangar, not stopping until he stood in her open doorway. She sat before her computer, a pencil between her teeth, muttering to herself. She glanced up at him in surprise, snatching the pencil from her mouth. The phone rang. Blushing, she grabbed at it. Then answered three more calls in quick succession, sending him an apologetic glance.

On the last call, an irate man's voice came clearly through, demanding payment for some overdue bill. "You know, what people are saying is right," the voice said loudly and rudely to Sami over the line, making Dillon frown at his harsh tone. "You'll never be able to recover from the stigma of that accident. You'll be hearing from our attorney."

Sami spoke to him calmly and quietly. She hung up and stared at her desk. Dillon couldn't care less about Reed's reputation. But he'd learned two things in the past five minutes that he hadn't been prepared for. One, the company faced serious financial disaster as a direct result from Kevin's accident, and two, Sami worked her tail off.

Despite his preconceived notions of how Old Man Reed had run the place, he had to face facts. Sami worked hard, fast, and efficiently, and he appreciated those qualities in anyone. He looked at her sitting in her chair, her eyes lit with embarrassment . . . and awareness. The most astonishing surge of pure, undiluted lust he'd ever experienced jolted through him. It shocked him into saying stupidly, "Guess your payables need work, huh?"

Her eyes turned wary. "You could say that."

His smile was wry as his body struggled to control its response to her. As wonderful as his family had been, neither his mother nor his father had ever mastered such a domestic chore as bill paying. "You get those calls often?"

"More than I'd like," she admitted, and Dillon was oddly disturbed at the thought.

"Did you want something?"

He didn't miss how quickly she'd recovered. So she could look wary and vulnerable, so what? She now wore a distant expression that clearly said *back off.* He couldn't let himself get fooled by her exterior, not when she could be the mastermind behind Kevin's death.

"I hoped you had a spare filing cabinet somewhere," he lied in a carefully neutral voice. "I'll need a place to store my files."

"There're several in the hangar. I'll show you." He followed her. The pretty floral dress she wore had a modest cut, but it still didn't hide her long and shapely body. Every slight breeze in the hangar tossed her dress about her knees, giving him an occasional glimpse of those trim thighs. She stopped and their gazes met. Again, Dillon felt that jolt as his body reacted. She looked away first, obviously flustered, then pointed out the spare office equipment lined up against one steel wall. He moved up behind her, though his thoughts were far from metal file cabinets.

"You can take whatever you need," she said.

"Can I?" he asked quietly, feeling intoxicated by the soft, clean scent of her.

She whirled around. Wariness lurked in her amber

eyes. She had no reason to be leery of him, and yet she was. He wanted to know why. He wanted to know what she hid, and as shocking as it was, he wanted her to confide in him.

He'd come to Reed Aviation with the intent of finding his brother's murderer. He'd expected to deal with Howard Reed. Under those circumstances, he would have had to be sneaky, conniving, and manipulative as hell. He now dealt with Sami, and he knew it would take very different measures. He didn't want to have to resort to getting his information behind her back. He wanted her willingly to tell him what he wanted to know.

And he had some intriguing ideas on exactly how he'd accomplish that.

TWO

"What did that man mean about an accident tarnishing Reed's reputation?" Dillon asked Sami suddenly.

He stood uncomfortably close to her. She could see nothing of the hangar past his wide shoulders, only him. His clear eyes unnerved her, as did his questions.

"There was an accident here about six months ago. One of our mechanics was testing a customer's plane and it crashed." Her heart ached. It remained unbelievably difficult to talk about sweet, lovable Kevin without pain. "He died."

Dillon went unnaturally still. Since the rest was no secret, she said, "The client, Clark Viewmont, pulled his other planes out. Then other longtime clients left too."

He didn't move a muscle. "That's when you closed the doors," he said, his voice low and controlled, and nearly inaudible in the noisy hangar.

"Yes." Without meaning to, she responded to his intensity, and the two of them stood still, the wind whistling around them. "My father had his first heart attack shortly after the accident."

"The accident was investigated."

She wondered at his intense interest. "Of course. The wreckage was so badly burned, no investigator ever agreed on the cause. Since we couldn't prove otherwise, the word got out that we were at fault."

"Meaning pilot error?"

He looked grim, even stoic, but she wasn't prepared for his fierce denial when she nodded.

"That's impossible." His voice didn't raise, but it was tight, curt, and very angry.

"How do you know?" she asked, taking an involuntary step back.

Dillon abruptly broke eye contact and nodded to the file cabinet against the wall. "I meant, those will be impossible to move by myself."

"Oh." She glanced from his hard face to the steel cabinets lined against the wall, confused by the sudden change of subject. No, she corrected, over the sudden change in *Dillon.* Just a minute before he'd been attentive, even friendly. Now he was completely withdrawn and distant, as if his thoughts were thousands of miles away.

The distinct drone of a small plane incoming on the runway caught their attention at the same time.

"Clark Viewmont," she said when she saw the tail number.

"The client whose plane was destroyed in the accident?"

Now why did he have that sudden canary-in-the-cat's-mouth look on his face? "The same," she said carefully, watching as another man exited with Clark.

"Ricardo. That's our head mechanic." They watched the man built like a linebacker walk beside Clark. "He starts up here again on Monday."

"Sami." Clark reached for her hand several feet before he came to a stop in front of her. A slender man in his forties, Clark reminded Sami of a turtle because of his long, slender neck, something she knew he wouldn't appreciate. He worked out faithfully and dressed from the pages of *GQ* magazine. When she didn't take his outstretched hand, his eyes hardened slightly, though his smile never faded. "A pleasure," he said in a cultured voice.

Reluctantly, she made the introductions, then turned to Clark. "We're still closed."

She felt his gaze slide over her and she managed not to shudder in revulsion. "Just wanted to say hello."

She acknowledged Ricardo's helpless shrug. He had, out of lack of work at Reed, been working at Mountain Aircraft. Ricardo had the reputation of being the best aircraft mechanic in the state, so she was pleased he'd be back.

Clark turned sharp eyes to Sami. "Your father isn't happy about the charter business, Sami."

So he'd been the one to leak the news of the charter to her father. "He would be, if people stopped bothering him about work. I've got a meeting, Clark. Did you want something in particular?"

"Just to see if you'll be opening on schedule."

"Why?"

"Maybe I'm tired of Mountain Aircraft. Maybe I want to land here again. Keep my planes here."

She should have been flattered. Would have been, if

she trusted him. His gaze scanned the empty hangar. "No planes."

The thought of all his money should have pleased her. "Not yet. But there will be." Dammit, she sounded defensive. She forced a deep breath. "You'll have to excuse me."

Clark stared first at her, then at Dillon, who didn't blink an eye. Once again, Sami was struck by how absolutely coiled and prepared Dillon seemed. Prepared for what, she couldn't imagine.

"See you Monday, Sami," Ricardo said quietly, following Clark to his plane.

Sami breathed a sigh of relief. The tension between Clark and Dillon had been unbearable. But why?

Monday morning, Reed's first official open day, Dillon and Ricardo walked slowly around Dillon's plane, checking every last detail for Kinley Charters' maiden flight. Dillon could have done it himself, but he had a feeling Ricardo might be a wealth of information. "Thanks for the time, Ricardo. I know you're busy."

"No problem," the soft-spoken man responded. "We go first-come, first-serve here. You're first." He was a large man, not as tall as Dillon, but much beefier, and had a roughness to him that belied his subdued, amiable attitude.

"We might have had our own charter, but the accident killed our reputation," he said.

"And a human being." Why didn't anyone ever mention that? Dillon carefully unfisted his hands and forced himself to relax. He wanted to talk about Kevin, wanted to hear about his last days. Had he laughed a lot? Played pranks? Flirted with anything in a skirt? Missed his brother? He wanted him back, dammit.

He saw the familiar plane coming down the runway. Clark Viewmont's plane. "Why would *he* come here?"

Ricardo glanced around. "Probably needs fuel. Or a service. We are an airport you know, and our prices are lower than Mountain Aircraft."

The radio on his hip crackled noisily. "Ricardo?"

"Who's that?" Dillon asked, knowing the wispy voice wasn't Sami's.

"Sami's secretary." Ricardo brought the radio to his lips. "Go, Lucy."

"Viewmont needs servicing."

"Got it." He clipped the radio back to his belt. "It'd be great for business if he's interested in coming back. Him and Old Man Reed were tight."

"What about his daughter?" It was hard, Dillon found, to keep his voice level when discussing Sami. He'd seen the way Viewmont had devoured her with his eyes, and for reasons he didn't understand, it had made him want to throttle the man.

"Sami?" Ricardo laughed softly. "Nah. They don't seem to like each other much."

Dillon wasn't sure he liked the puppy-dog infatuation he saw swimming in Ricardo's eyes, but before he had time to analyze his strange preoccupation with how people looked at Sami Reed, Ricardo's radio spit again.

"Ricardo?" Sami's voice crackled with authority. "Viewmont needs servicing. Now."

"I've got two planes in maintenance," Ricardo told her, but she had already clicked off without another word.

"So much for first-come, first-serve," Dillon said ironically. And so much for honesty and integrity.

Ricardo shrugged and walked off, whistling.

Dillon heard her heels clicking steadily through the hangar long before he caught a glimpse of her. She was walking away from him, toward the lobby. No dress today. In its place was a lace blouse tucked into trim, tailored trousers that made him realize she didn't need a skirt to show off those thoroughbred legs.

Suddenly, she stopped and turned.

Across at least eighty feet their gazes met. Neither moved. The strange urge to touch her nearly overwhelmed him. She felt it, too, he could see it as her body swayed slightly toward his. Abruptly, she turned away, then entered the lobby.

Dillon followed her, not sure if he wanted to discuss her unfair business policies, or if, despite himself, he just needed to see her again.

Sami glanced up during her phone conversation. Dillon filled her doorway, that built body radiating heat and power. She swiveled her chair so he couldn't see her face, and the confusion she knew was all over it.

"Does your doctor know you're calling?" she asked her father, intensely aware of Dillon behind her, soaking up every word.

"No," her father admitted. "Clark wants back, Sami. I want you to cater to him for now."

"Why?"

"Please, Sami. Just do this for me."

She heard Dillon shift restlessly behind her, but

didn't dare look at him. She was human enough, and she absolutely didn't need the distraction of his annoyingly beautiful eyes right now.

She hesitated, unable to promise to be nice to Clark Viewmont. "I need to talk to you. Why—"

"Not now. The nurse is coming." The phone went dead.

"Does he run this place from his hospital bed?"

Irritation replaced the weariness she'd felt only seconds before. Was it really so strange that a woman wanted to run the company? That one could? She stood up and purposely walked passed him to her filing cabinet, where she slowly returned a fat manila file to its place. "What do you want?"

He didn't answer, and she slid the drawer shut, spun back toward him, and stifled a startled gasp. He stood an inch from her, over six feet of tough, rangy masculinity. Those eyes mesmerized, pulled and attracted, but why, she couldn't guess. She backed up a step and felt the cold cabinet against her legs. He put his large hands against the drawers on either side of her head and leaned in.

"*What do I want?*" he repeated huskily, his eyes veiled by his long, dark lashes. "Now there's a question."

The closeness should have frightened her, but it only excited. Her heart raced and an unaccustomed warmth stole through her. When was the last time a man had done that to her? Never, she admitted. She clasped her hands together nervously since the only other place to put them was on Dillon. He was so tall, she had to lean back against the cabinet to see his face, then her breath caught at his softened expression. The newfound warmth quickly turned to goose bumps.

"How about it, Sami? Do you want the same thing I want?"

That gaze held her. His clean white shirt stretched taut across broad shoulders. A faint woodsy scent wafted up from his skin. When her tongue darted out to nervously lick her lips, his eyes followed the motion. She tingled everywhere. Her every nerve hummed with pressure as her fingers curled against the cold metal behind her back.

"Do you?" he whispered. His gaze was hungry and hot, waiting. He tilted his head toward hers. Her lips parted, in anticipation, in panic.

Her intercom buzzed, and she jumped. He stayed still. When it buzzed insistently again, she brushed past him, striving desperately for composure. "Yes?"

"Clark wants to see you." Ricardo's sympathetic voice echoed through the room.

Dillon's expression darkened, and Sami wondered whether it was the untimely interruption or the request. Either way, those light sea-green eyes once again hid his every thought. Could she have imagined that brief tenderness and sharp longing she'd seen only seconds before? It seemed likely.

"Excuse me," she said to Dillon, who watched her silently. "I've got to see a customer."

"I thought his plane burned."

Her heart twisted at the reminder of Kevin. "He bought another."

"So he gets preferential treatment."

The new expression on his face defied description,

but one thing she knew for certain. It didn't come close to resembling tenderness or longing. "No. Of course not."

"You're lying."

Sami couldn't be sure which hurt most—being called a liar, or being called that by a man who was beginning to fascinate her.

Without a word, she moved toward the door.

Dillon had learned to read her annoyance level by the decibel level of her shoes on the floor. They clicked very loudly now. "Your mechanic drops everything he's working on to make Clark Viewmont happy. Why, Sami?"

She stopped at the door, gripping the jamb as if she needed the support. "That's none of your business."

"Why, Sami?" he pushed.

"I just want him out of here," she said, so softly he could hardly hear her.

Dillon wanted to doubt her. He wanted to think she was playing him for a fool, but he couldn't. Something flickered through those soft, topaz eyes of hers, and it didn't look like deceit. It came straight from the heart.

It was sheer honesty, so genuine he could feel it. She turned from him and walked out, and this time he let her go.

Sami walked into the lobby. Felicia, her receptionist, pointed to Clark. Sami nodded but didn't return the smile. Felicia had a terrible tendency to gossip, and she didn't want to give the fire fuel. She would have hired someone new long ago, but for some reason her father insisted the woman stay.

"I'm busy, Clark. What is it?"

"You've lost a lot of customers," he noted casually.

"We've gained some new ones."

"Not all that many, Sami. You must be hurting."

Why had her father wanted her to be nice to this man? "What's your point, Clark?"

He shrugged. "I could help."

"No, thanks."

His eyes lost some of their friendliness. "You can't afford to turn me down. Your father wouldn't like that decision."

So he'd tell her father. Frustration welled up within her, tinged with desperation. Her father couldn't take any more disappointment. "I'll give you five minutes."

She turned, intending for Clark to follow her to her office. She didn't need Felicia repeating every word to whoever would listen. But she got another unpleasant surprise. Dillon leaned against the wall, not five feet from her, unabashedly eavesdropping. His face was a solid mask of inscrutable stone. She had no idea what thoughts ran through his head as his cool eyes rested impassively on her, but one thing was certain. It wasn't the heat and longing of several minutes ago.

"Sami." He completely ignored Clark. He pushed away from the doorway and straightened to his considerable height. In Clark's overdone suit, he looked like a little boy playing dress-up next to Dillon's sheer size and understated pilot's uniform of a starched white shirt, navy trousers, and suspenders.

She and Clark walked past him on their way to her office. She could feel his eyes on her. They made her hot and cold at the same time. He took such interest in her. Business or personal? And why?

Dillon made sure to pass Sami in the lobby after his flight. Not surprising, she kept walking, ignoring him. He simply changed directions to keep pace with her, noticing the pale purple shadows under her eyes. She looked tired. And sexy. "Where's Viewmont?"

"Gone."

She sounded relieved. Real emotion, he wondered, or an act? "You think he's a jerk," he ventured.

"What I think of him is none of your business." She kept walking.

"You do," he insisted.

She said nothing but increased her pace. Those heels of hers rang pleasantly with each step and the soft sway of her hips momentarily distracted him. Together they left the lobby, and though Dillon didn't know their destination, he followed her through hangar one and into hangar two.

"What are you doing?" She frowned.

"Talking to you," he said evenly, opening a door for her when she came to a stop in front of it. The small storage area was filled with metal racks, each loaded with what looked like spare airplane parts. "Inventory?" he asked.

"Yes." She hesitated in front of one of the huge units, her eyes scanning the shelves.

"You aren't going to tell me what he wanted, are you?"

She looked at him. "Why does Clark concern you at all?"

"He doesn't concern you?" Damn her, how had she

turned the tables on him? He was the one who needed answers, he was the one working an investigation.

"Of course he does—" She clamped her mouth shut, as if to keep her words to herself.

She didn't want to reveal too much, he thought bitterly. And he so desperately needed to know. Suddenly, the urge to tell her about Kevin was strong, to beg for information if he had to. But if she wouldn't tell him now, she sure as hell wouldn't tell him after she found out he'd lied to her.

He cursed himself for noticing things like how lovely she looked in her neat, fitted trousers that emphasized her long legs, how she lit the room with her mere presence. How her breath caught every time she looked at him.

"If you're unhappy," she said, "break your lease."

"Maybe I like the services you're offering."

Irritated, she stepped back. "Why do you do that?"

"Do what?" he asked innocently.

"Turn everything into a sexual innuendo."

He smiled slyly. "I don't do that, Sami. *You* do."

She turned from him.

"If Reed Aviation was responsible for the destruction of Viewmont's precious plane, why did he come back? What are you offering him that Mountain Aircraft isn't?"

"Cheaper prices on fuel. Better mechanics. Besides, this is only his second time back."

Unsatisfied, frustrated, he looked around them at the small, stuffy room. "What are we doing here?"

"Looking for a part that Clark swears is in here. Ricardo's swamped, I promised to come find it." She reached for a heavy part off the second to top shelf. "Here it is—"

"Don't!" Dillon shouted too late. The entire rack of shelves started to pull away from the wall, and with it, a shower of sharp metal parts and boxes rained down on them.

THREE

Acting on pure survival instinct that had been well-sharpened over his years in the military, Dillon dove at Sami, his first and only thought to protect. His velocity had them flying against the wall. Something sharp and painful hit his shoulder as it fell. Lifting his arms around Sami, he shielded her from the flying debris as best he could, but still he felt her jerk beneath him as something scraped her. Behind them, the entire shelving unit crashed to the floor.

He still held her close, even when silence reigned, amazingly reluctant to let go. Her hair tickled his nose. His hands spread wide over her slender back to touch all he could. She pushed away from him, looking shaken. Coughing at the thick cloud of dirt, she stared in wonder at the mess that lay at their feet.

"You okay?" he demanded, lifting her chin with a finger to inspect her face. A small smudge of dirt streaked her cheek. A little scratch lined one side of her neck. No blood.

"Yes." She closed her eyes at his touch, which for

some reason made his blood surge. Dust rose ominously from the huge unit on the floor. Parts littered the floor. "How about you?"

"Peachy." He touched the heavy unit with his toe and whistled softly, shaking his head. "That could have crushed our skulls nicely."

Her wide gaze landed on his. "I—" She stopped abruptly. "That was close."

He rolled his aching shoulder and let out a wry laugh. "That was a little more than close, Sami." Even totally shaken, she was incredibly beautiful. He'd seen plenty of beautiful women before, but never one that distracted him so damn much. This one made him forget things—like the unlikeliness of what had just happened. Could the whole thing have been contrived to take him off guard? No, he decided. She had no idea what he was up to. She couldn't.

So why was she looking at him with such hesitation?

His gut tightened uncomfortably. He wanted, badly, to believe this had been an accident. "I guess you owe me a thank you."

She looked at him then. "Yes, I do. Thank—" She stopped abruptly, as if she'd just heard the slight sarcasm.

"Come on," he taunted. Near-death experiences tended to bring out the worst in him. "Can't you think of a better way to thank me than that?"

"You're disgusting." She turned, tripping over a fallen part in her haste to escape him. And for as long as he could hear them, he stood listening to the fading sound of her pounding heels as she hurried from him.

◆——————◆

Sami loved the airport at night. Standing against the windows in the lobby, with the lights off all around her, she watched the stars make their trail across the night. Normally, the luxury of being all alone thrilled her.

But she couldn't stop thinking about the business, her father, and Dillon. At least he'd been so busy with his charter, their paths had barely crossed in two days. Ricardo had been horrified at the accident. No one but mechanics were allowed in the room now, and Sami had tried to forget the incident.

But she couldn't do the same for the letter she'd gotten in the mail that day. Just as before, she had no clue as to the sender. *Kevin didn't have to die.* A prank? She hoped so.

The last few days had been a whirlwind of activity. The good news—Reed Aviation buzzed with business. The not so good news—most of that activity came from Kinley Charters. No doubt, she appreciated it, but had decided it was a mixed blessing.

Dillon confused her. She'd avoided men for so long, it had become a habit. She wasn't used to someone so . . . masculine, someone so overtly sexual. She sighed into the silent, darkened lobby. A soft footstep behind her made her jump in alarm.

Dillon appeared out of the shadows and just looked at her.

"You startled me." Nothing new. If she walked through the hangar, she saw him. If she thought she was alone, he stepped out from nowhere. He was everywhere, all the time, and he seemed inexplicably interested in her private affairs. Her imagination? Staring now into his strong, captivating features, she didn't think so.

She thought of a conversation she'd overheard between Lucy and Felicia in front of the coffee machine. They were both fascinated by Dillon, and they'd been discussing his past. She shouldn't have been surprised to know that the enigmatic man who spent so much time on her mind affected her employees the same way. She'd learned that he'd started flying when he'd been just a kid, fighting forest fires from the air. He'd been a test pilot for the Air Force, too, flying planes no one even knew were flyable. Apparently, Dillon Kinley did it all.

Looking at him now, with his dangerous eyes and unreadable expression, Sami could indeed believe him capable of anything.

"You startle easy," he said. "Is it me? Are you afraid of me?"

"Of course not." They stared at each other.

"We're not friends, are we?" he asked solemnly.

She was attracted, no question. Reason enough to avoid him. "No," she agreed. "We're not friends."

He stepped closer, slipped his hands into his pockets, and turned to the window where she'd been standing. "Why is that?"

A tough one, she thought. And getting tougher with every passing moment. He squared his shoulders, and the leather jacket he wore over his pilot's uniform crinkled with a soft, giving sound. His expression seemed grim, making him appear too serious, darkly dangerous . . . immensely appealing. And he wanted to know why they weren't friends. "Maybe I don't like men without a sense of humor."

Those expressive eyebrows leaped upward, insulted. "I have a great sense of humor."

She shot him a level look. Not with her, he didn't. "Yeah? Try showing it sometime."

"Fair enough." His lips curved slightly, and he reached out to stroke her neck with a careful finger. "But wouldn't you know it, I'm fresh out of jokes now."

Oh, great. So he could be compassionate and funny as well as intelligent and charming. She stepped back from the glorious view of the night sky and turned away. There was no telling what could happen to her inhibitions on a night like this. "I've got to go."

He stepped in her way, his eyes probing. "I didn't mean to chase you away. You've been busy."

She leaned back against the glass wall and gave him a self-deprecatory smile. "Thanks to you."

He leaned back, too, his shoulder brushing against hers. She felt oddly connected to him. The lobby stretched out in front of them, quiet and dark. "If you hate this so much, why do you do it?"

"I don't hate it. I love it," she said in surprise, pushing away from the wall to stare at him. "Why would you think I didn't?"

"I don't know." He stood up too. "Maybe because you always seem to be weighed under by the stress of it all." He walked around the lobby, restlessly running fingers over leather couches, marble tables. "I've never seen you laugh—which is curious considering Ricardo says you've got a great sense of humor. But mostly, you just don't seem . . ." He turned to look at her. "Well, happy."

She hadn't thought about it, but she did so now. She didn't know if it was the shock of the letters, or the strain of keeping her father happy. Or maybe she still mourned the loss of Kevin. But he was right, and it was unsettlingly perceptive of him to notice when no one else had. "I'm fine."

He looked away. "Shouldn't you be home by now, going out with your friends or something?"

She laughed. "Something, as in a date?"

"Yeah," he said softly, bringing his gaze back to hers. "You work nearly every night, far after everyone else leaves. When do you have fun?"

Fun. Oh, she believed in it, she just never seemed to have time for it. Before this job, she'd had another high-stress job, in charge of starting up a new system and acclimating two hundred and fifty employees to the computer life. And before that, college, where she'd completed her undergraduate and then her master's degree in just five years. Maybe that's why she could count on one hand the number of relationships she'd had in her entire life. Make that one finger. Her innate wariness around men didn't help, and few had bothered to try to get past the emotional barrier she'd constructed.

Few, until Dillon Kinley.

"I manage to work fun in," she said discreetly. She did have friends, she thought defensively. Some were even men. But that's all they were—just friends.

"Are you busy right now?"

"No," she said cautiously.

He chuckled, and the sound had her stomach doing a slow, sensuous roll. "You're a suspicious thing. Well, good. You're free. So we can talk business."

"It's after hours." Why had Ricardo told him she had a sense of humor? What else had he said? And why was he looking at her that way? As if . . . she amused him?

"So much the better." He hit her with that irresistible smile that could knock her knees weak. "This way, I have your undivided attention."

As if he'd ever had anything less. "For what?"

"What I want to know is, how can a place like this," he gestured about him and his luxurious surroundings, "afford to run on its antiquated systems and business practices."

She'd asked her father often enough, so why was she so surprised he'd been intelligent enough to ask the same of her? If only she had a satisfactory answer to give him.

He walked toward the reception desk and flipped on a neat little lamp that set a glow over the desk. "Everything is so new and lush."

"They need to be appealing."

"True enough. But let's be realistic, Sami. Your fuel trucks are constantly down for repairs, your mechanics don't keep an inventory of parts on hand because of the cost, and you don't even keep a line crew on duty twenty-four hours a day unless you know you have an incoming flight." He picked up the previous day's fuel sales report from Felicia's desk. "See? Nothing for yesterday. The big zip, Sami. Why?" He looked at her.

She chewed her lip and turned away. He knew damn well why.

"Because both trucks were down," he said with a shake of his head. "We all had to scramble elsewhere for fuel. Not only is that incredibly inconvenient, it's very unwise. I'll bet three out of four of those pilots that came through here yesterday won't be needing fuel next time they come. They'll fuel at their previous stop." He tossed down the report with disgust.

She could tell him that her research had shown it was no longer economical to own her own fuel trucks. She had successfully arranged for the leasing of three new trucks, but they wouldn't arrive until next week due to some sort of shipping delay. She could tell him that it didn't pay to keep an inventory on hand for her mechanics because they dealt with so many different kinds of aircraft daily. It was far cheaper and more efficient for them to order on an as-needed basis. And she'd just hired additional crew, who starting next week would be working around the clock.

She could tell him all of that. She simply didn't have the energy.

Dillon flipped off the lamp, sending them back into darkness. He perched a hip against the desk and crossed his arms. Again, the leather slid together, making that sound that seemed so utterly masculine. "No comment?"

She opened her mouth to retort, but he interrupted her by placing a finger over her lips. "I know, don't tell me. It's none of my business."

She lifted her eyebrows but didn't move. She couldn't. His gaze held her. Something funny happened to her insides. When she finally exhaled under his fingers, she was close enough to see his eyes darken, his chest rise with his deep breath. His fingers slid over her cheek and around her nape, gently cupping her head. Staring at her intently, he pulled her closer, his eyes boring into hers.

"Dillon—"

"Shhh." He touched her lips with his, in a quick,

soft kiss that sent her senses reeling. Her body leaned into him, craving, yearning, but he withdrew his hand and pulled back.

"Good night," he whispered. Then he walked away.

Sami sat in the dark for a long time after that, bewildered and confused. *He'd kissed her.* And incredible as it seemed, she wanted another.

All the way to his Jeep, and then all the way to the cabin he'd rented, Dillon crucified himself for that damn kiss. He'd known he was going to do it the minute he saw her standing under the windows, looking as completely alone as he felt.

His hands fisted against the steering wheel as he maneuvered the narrow two-lane mountain road. He was thirty-two years old, not some over-hormoned teenager, so what was wrong with him? Yet, he knew.

Despite all the years alone, he wasn't a loner at heart. Loving and being loved in return was natural for him. But his loved ones had been ripped from him prematurely, freezing those feelings and emotions.

The defrosting hurt.

This hopeless attraction to the one female he *had* to stay away from made it even more so. But acknowledging the problem was easy—doing something about it would be another thing entirely.

"You . . . *what?*"

Sami winced and hunched in her chair to drop her head to her desk. From over the phone she could hear her father's heart monitor bleep warningly.

"Relax, Dad," she pleaded. "There was no reason to tell you I'd turned down Clark's proposal. And Clark shouldn't have told you either."

"Well, I'm glad he did. Do you have any idea how much money he's worth to us?"

Her chair squeaked as she rolled restlessly behind her desk. "I never told him he couldn't use our regular services. I just told him he couldn't house himself here again as a tenant."

"Why, for God's sake?"

"His demands were too high. He wanted to have all of hangar one—free. He wanted his fuel guaranteed at ten cents a gallon lower than our posted price, and he wanted the mechanics at his beck and call. What kind of a deal is that?"

"Sami, we've *always* given him his fuel cheap—he buys *thousands* of gallons at a time," he protested. "And as far as our mechanics, they can do what we tell them to do or take a hike."

She held her breath on that one. She wished she could make her father believe that employee morale was one of the most important things to a successful business—and you couldn't have it without basic respect. On both sides.

"And," he continued, "we have plenty of office space available."

Not anymore, she thought. Not since Kinley Charters. Her father's disappointment hurt. All she'd ever wanted was his admiration and approval, but she was old enough to know she could run her life just fine without it. Or that's what she kept telling herself. "It's unethical to give Clark his fuel cheaper than our other regular customers, and while I'm in charge, I refuse to do so," she said carefully, refusing to back down. "And our mechanics are working on a first-come, first-serve basis. It keeps the order and our customers happy."

"You're disobeying me?"

She could hear the astonishment. The need to give in nearly overwhelmed her. But she was no longer an easily frightened child. She wanted to please him more than almost anything, just not at the risk of her beliefs. "You put me in charge of this company because you trusted me."

"If you'd cater to Viewmont, you'd triple your success story," he said, sounding resigned.

"Cater?"

Lucy came in, her purse slung over her shoulder.

"Giving in to Clark's needs can be . . . rewarding," he said carefully.

"One of your mechanics died giving in to his needs," she reminded him. Lucy stilled and Sami sent her an apologetic look. She knew that Lucy had harbored secret romantic feelings for Kevin, and that she still grieved.

"I'm well aware that one of my employees died, Sami," her father said unevenly. "Our insurance canceled us. Remember?"

Her throat tightened. "Tell me Kevin's death meant more to you than that."

"Of course it did." He sighed again. "I'm just having a hard time being so idle."

Compassion welled inside her, but so did frustration. "Why do you feel so loyal to Clark?"

"He's . . . a friend. Please, Sami, do this for me."

She refused to promise anything. They hung up, and Sami sank into her desk chair, rubbing her eyes.

"Rough day, huh?" Lucy asked softly, her voice low with concern.

"You could say so." She forced a smile. "Thanks for your work on the fuel reports. I couldn't have finished them without you."

Lucy shrugged. "I don't mind the overtime. It keeps my mind off . . . things."

Kevin. "I can give you some time off if—"

"No," she said quickly, with a sharp shake of her pretty red head. "Time off only makes it worse. Work has been good, Sami."

"Well, that's a relief," Sami said with a smile. "I was half-afraid you'd take me up on my offer." She pushed back from her desk. "You're on your way out now, I see. Good night."

Lucy stood and moved to the door. "Jim and his wife are having a party. You deserve a night off."

She couldn't afford a night off. There was too much to do, too much to think about. She felt if she so much as let her guard down for a second, she'd lose control of the tenuous grip she had on the business. "I'm sorry, Lucy. I can't."

Lucy's footsteps echoed down the deserted hallway until Sami was completely alone—alone with her thoughts, her troubles, her loneliness. It was at times like this when she missed her mother most. Two years she'd been gone from cancer, but it seemed like forever. But even if she could talk to her mother, what would she say? That her father was not exactly as loving and open as she'd expected? Debbie Reed had no illusions where her ex-husband was concerned. Hadn't Sami heard that often enough growing up?

Sami sighed. She had plenty to be thankful for. She

was running a business she absolutely loved. She loved the airplanes, loved the constant flow of new people, loved the challenge. So things weren't perfect. The accident had dealt them a serious blow. The employees were still devastated, customers still a little nervous.

And then there was Dillon. He'd kissed her, but she knew he hadn't been pleased about it. She'd seen his dark look when he'd lifted his lips from hers, just before he'd stalked off into the night. Well, she thought, he'd confused her often enough, it was about time she got to do the same thing to him.

She pulled out the two letters she'd received and flattened them out on her desk. She'd give anything to know what had really happened to Kevin in those last few moments. He'd had a real talent for flying, so one thing remained certain in her mind.

It hadn't been pilot error.

"Working hard?"

Sami nearly leaped out of her skin at the deep, familiar voice. A pair of work-roughened hands planted themselves firmly on her desk, effectively trapping her letters beneath them, as he leaned close to her.

Her heart slammed against her ribs as she tried to pull the letters out from beneath his hands. "Excuse me," she said, panicked. She wasn't ready for anyone else to see them.

But Dillon had set those disconcerting green eyes of his on her, scrutinizing as if he'd caught *her* snooping instead of the other way around. "What's the matter?" he asked, lifting his hands. "You looked funny."

She scooped up the two sheets of paper and clasped them to her chest. "I'm . . . just working."

He tilted his head toward her as he tended to do

when she wouldn't look at him. She felt like squirming. "A little jittery for someone who's just working," he said finally.

The way the man could annoy her at the same time he accelerated her pulse really topped the cake. "I'm busy, Dillon. Did you need something?"

He seemed to see right through her. "What's wrong?"

He was butting in again, but being upset always slowed her reflexes. Just a few more minutes between her phone call to her father and Dillon's arrival—and she could have been back in control. She pressed the letters to her and cursed herself for not leaving earlier. "Nothing's wrong."

He came around her desk, and she pushed back in her chair. "What's the matter?" he repeated, frowning as he bore down on her. "Another set of shelves fall on you?"

The reminder of that coming on the heels of reading the letters again had her paling. "No."

He reached for her hands.

"Hey!" She tried to swivel away.

Cursing softly, he held the chair firmly in place with his legs and slowly, methodically, pried her fingers away from the letters. They struggled until he took her wrist in his strong fingers and pressed. Instantly numb, her fingers relaxed, and he took the papers.

"Damn you!" she said with a gasp, shaking her wrist.

"I'm sorry." But the glitter in his eyes had nothing to do with apology, and though he'd obviously been very careful not to hurt her, it still galled that he'd muscled his way with her.

"Where did you learn that?" she demanded.

His smile was grim, completely without mirth. "Believe me, you don't want to know." He lifted the letters up to read them.

"No!" She struggled, but she was no match for someone who had never fought by the rules.

He merely straightened to his full height and held the papers up out of reach, peering at her strangely, almost as if he were worried. But that was crazy, she reasoned, he didn't care about her.

"I've never seen you like this before," he said in a low, controlled voice. "You're white as a sheet—" He cut himself off as he caught a glimpse of the first message. Quickly, he flipped to the second while she gripped the arms of her chair, furious.

"Those are mine," she said fiercely. "And you have no right to manhandle me—"

Her own words faded away as he blanched beneath his tan and dropped the letters on her desk. With jerky movements, he backed to a chair and collapsed into it as if he needed the support. "Where did those come from?"

"I—You're shaking, Dillon."

He gripped the arms of the chair, rigid with tension. "Answer the question, Sami."

"Why does it matter so much to you?"

"Dammit. Just answer me. *Who sent them?*" He enunciated each word through clenched teeth. No warmth remained in his hard, angry face. He stood stiffly, looking surprisingly menacing, tough and ready for battle.

Sami stared at him in surprise, still adjusting to the change from compassion to fury. She didn't think he'd hurt her, but didn't feel like taking any chances. Not when he was looking at her with a barely restrained violence. She dashed to the door, knowing everyone else had left long ago.

"I asked you a question," he grated out. A muscle ticked in his cheek, but he didn't make another move toward her.

From the safety of the office door she turned, feeling a burst of courage. "It's none of your business." Anger had replaced her fear. "And I resent you barging in here, bulldozing your way around and reading my personal property."

She knew if he'd really wanted to, nothing would have stopped him from getting the answers he wanted from her. That he didn't force the issue came as small comfort. He shook with anger.

"If these letters mean what I think they mean," he bit out, "then you're obstructing justice. Do you understand what I'm saying? You're breaking the law. So come back here and explain them, or I'll call the police."

FOUR

"I got them in the mail," Sami said, still gripping the doorway, braced to run fast and hard. "And I'm not hiding them," she added, slightly defensive. "They were addressed to me and marked personal."

"Come back in here," Dillon said quietly, softening his expression, relieved she was about to tell him what she knew. He'd scared her to death, though he really hadn't meant to. She had no way of knowing how important the letters were to him. "I won't bite."

She shook her head and rubbed her wrist again, making him feel like a first-class jerk. He knew he hadn't hurt her because he was more than well-trained, but he still shouldn't have done it. "Sami, I'm sorry."

"No, you're not."

He gave her a little smile. "I'm sorry I scared you."

"But not that you barged in here and read something you shouldn't have."

She looked at him with those wide, gorgeous eyes and something inside him twitched. His regret grew. Why, he wondered, couldn't they be on the same side?

"Come here," he repeated quietly. "I promise I won't hurt you."

Those golden eyes searched his features carefully, and for some reason, he wanted badly for her to like what she saw. But evidently, he fell short of the mark. "No," she said, walking out.

She'd called his bluff. He could make grown men quiver in their boots with just a look, and she'd not blinked an eye. Well, so much for getting her to trust him and open up, he thought, disgusted with himself.

Something about that woman defused his defenses. Left him vulnerable. Maybe it was because when she moved with such fluidity, the blood drained from his head to his lap. Or when she spoke in that soft, cultured way of hers, he couldn't concentrate on anything but her lips.

She disturbed him all right, and he had the hard-on to prove it.

In his own office, he sat alone with his newest concern. What was going to happen when he proved what he hoped to prove? At this point, he could only hope he wouldn't discover Sami had been involved, but he knew, regardless, she wouldn't thank him for exposing it all. Why it mattered to him what that stubborn, temperamental woman thought of him, he didn't know. But it did. Too much.

Then he heard the distant clang. He rose, knowing it was too late for anything harmless. He stepped into the dark, quiet night and heard it again. Hangar three. It was the oldest and the only yet-unrenovated building at the airport, and as far as he knew it was never used.

He crossed the airstrip and tried the side door. It opened easily under his hand, surprising him. He'd poked his head in once and knew that a long hallway opened up into the hangar, with abandoned offices on either side. But he could see none of that now. The hallway was pitch-black. The flickering light ahead, where no one had any business being, had him sighing.

He crept softly down the hall, wondering what the hell he was getting himself into. By keeping a light hand on the wall, he knew when the hallway stopped and opened up to the huge hangar. But he also would have known by the sudden sense of yawning, gigantic space.

Then the light flickered again, obviously a flashlight, casting an eerie green glow about the metal walls. Dead silence prevailed, except for the soft whistling of the wind that brushed through the rafters high above. He moved forward.

And stopped short.

Sami was seated in the cockpit of an old crop duster biplane. Her head was back against the headrest, and she lay so still she could have been asleep. Except her face looked pale as death.

His shoes squeaked on the concrete floor as he ran toward her, his steps throwing a strange echo throughout the hangar. Her eyes flashed open as her head whipped blindly around in the dark. She shined the light down in his face.

"You!" She let her head fall back and lowered the light. "Didn't I say good night to you already?"

Without the light, they were cast in absolute darkness. "Maybe." He moved closer as his eyes adjusted quickly. He had to tip his head up to see her.

"Then what are you doing here?"

"I could ask you the same thing." He still reeled

from the vision of her deathly white face and far too
still body. "You gave me gray hairs on that one, Sami."

"Did I?"

"Yes, dammit. I thought you were hurt."

"And you came running to my rescue." She laughed
softly but completely without mirth. "That's touching,
Dillon. Go away."

He was close enough now to see that she still
wouldn't look at him. His patience was diminishing by
the minute. "What in the hell are you doing out here in
the dark? And all alone?"

She shrugged, and he got the gist of it. *None of your
business*, he could hear her say. His initial concern for
her had faded to be replaced by irritation, but the anxi-
ety hit him again when he caught a good look at her
face.

She'd been crying.

A woman's tears remained one of the only things
that could completely fluster the unflappable Dillon
Kinley. For the first time since he'd entered the hangar,
he felt like turning tail and running. But this was Sami
in front of him, fighting tears, and he found he couldn't
dismiss them.

"Come on," he cajoled up to her, knowing she'd
hate any sympathy, *especially* his. "Come down and I'll
let you take a swing at me. I know you want to." She
still had to explain those letters.

"Dillon." She sighed, her voice soft and raspy,
"What do you want from me?"

He wanted a whole hell of a lot of things. He
wanted to know if she was as lethal and ruthless as her
father. He wanted to know why she'd hidden the letters
about Kevin. But most of all, at that moment, he

wanted to know if the rest of her was as soft and giving as her lips had been the other night. "I want to talk to you," he said instead.

"I want to be alone." Her voice broke.

If he'd found his way into this deserted hangar, anyone could. "Get down," he said gently. "Or I'm coming up to get you."

She made a distressed sound and turned away, but he was done allowing her to call his bluff. The plane creaked and groaned as he hauled himself up and squeezed into the seat next to her. God, what a beauty, he thought, glancing around the cockpit. He ached to fly it.

"I don't know when the fuel trucks are going to arrive," she said dispassionately. "Or why the mechanics are behind. I don't know the schedule for tomorrow either, so don't ask me."

"Nice plane," he said, ignoring her tirade. "Is it yours?"

She blinked at him, then laughed. Dillon gaped at her in surprise as the sweet sound rolled over him. He couldn't remember hearing her laugh before. He found himself smiling back. "Wow. I didn't know you could do that." Strangely enough, he wanted to hear the infectious sound again.

She looked at him and . . . something happened. They weren't two business associates at constant odds over any given business practice. They weren't landlord and tenant, not in this moment anyway. They were just two people sitting in the dark, out in the middle of nowhere.

The force of the attraction hit Dillon like a two-fisted punch. Slowly, a little shaken, he reached out and stroked her neck. The contact of his warm hand on her cool skin sent shivers over the both of them, and beneath his fingers, her pulse tattooed out a frantic beat. His matched it. Slowly, he pulled her closer, meeting her halfway.

The kiss started out inquisitive and soft. Within seconds it escalated into a hard, wet, scorching connection that had them panting for breath and struggling for a better position within the tight confines of the cockpit.

Like everything she did, Sami kissed with an intense concentration and wild passion. It drove him nuts. Her flashlight clattered noisily between them, but the dark only fueled the fire. She made catchy little sounds deep in her throat that were the most incredibly sexy sounds he'd ever heard, and he yanked her closer, tighter, harder against him.

The dials and gadgets in the close cockpit gouged him every time he moved, making him curse in frustration. She laughed softly, then moaned when he gripped her head in fisted hands to hold her still, and devoured her sweet neck with wet, open-mouthed kisses. She pressed his face to her, holding him there.

It wasn't enough. He had to have more.

Through the clingy silk of her thin blouse, he cupped her breast, running his thumb over the hardened peak, willing to die of pleasure right there when she let out a startled gasp and dug her fingers hard into his arms. Dipping his head, he kissed her softly through the material, then unbuttoned her enough to draw it aside. A soft, flimsy scrap of a bra covered her, and he bent her back over his arm, closing his eyes as he inhaled her lovely scent. His tongue nudged aside the light barrier; then she was in his mouth, against his tongue, and his only thought was heaven couldn't be better.

"Oops," a voice exclaimed as a flash of light beamed directly on them. "Sorry."

Dillon let out a pithy curse, shielding Sami from the light. His still trembling fingers worked to right her clothes.

"Ricardo," Sami said with a gasp, shoving away from Dillon.

"Don't you ever go home?" Dillon, still rocked by the most powerful kiss he'd ever experienced in his life, found himself drowning in fury. He was as painfully erect as the steel of the plane that surrounded him—a damned uncomfortable feeling for several reasons, not the least of which was the stunned way Ricardo continued to stare at Sami.

Ricardo mumbled another apology, but he couldn't seem to stop looking at Sami's disheveled state, or at her hand, which was clenching her blouse together. Dillon, irritated beyond belief, swore again. He blocked Ricardo's view and fought with Sami's hands, winning, then buttoned her up.

"Didn't mean to interrupt anything," Ricardo said, unmistakably shaken. His gaze shifted off Sami, and his extraordinarily large hands shook as he jerked the light off her.

"You didn't," Sami assured him to Dillon's annoyance. Hell, she'd acted . . . guilty. Which only further irritated him.

What the hell did she have to feel guilty about? It was her airport, her plane, her life, unless . . . Had he read everything all wrong? Was Ricardo more than just the mechanic? Ricardo turned, shooting Sami one last, lingering look of disappointment before he walked away.

Neither Sami nor Dillon spoke. Less than a minute later, they heard the side door slam shut. Sami's slow exhale echoed around him. Jealousy, an emotion Dillon had never bothered to waste a second on, spread like wildfire through his limbs until he felt paralyzed with it. "You have something going on with Ricardo," he said flatly. Why hadn't he seen it before?

She denied it with a shake of her head. "It's just that . . . well . . ." She trailed off awkwardly.

Dillon waited, but as seemed typical, she didn't explain further. "Don't strain yourself on my account coming up with excuses for doing your mechanic."

"Why, you—"

He held up a finger warningly. "Careful. I'm your only paying tenant."

"You're conceited beyond belief." She shoved back the hair from her eyes and rubbed her temples, her shoulders bent forward.

And dammit if she didn't look suddenly so vulnerable that his arms didn't itch for her. It made him angry all over again. He struggled for the calm and finesse he'd decided she needed. "Let's talk."

She made a sound, then straightened and gave him her suspicious, on-guard look. "*Talk?*"

"Yeah, talk. You do that real well with others, I noticed. Not so well with me."

Her eyes narrowed. "It's hard to talk to a Neanderthal."

His grin was genuine, and suddenly affable. Call

him sick, but he did love to banter with her. "Okay, we'll do this another way. *I'll* talk and you answer."

"I'm not going to answer questions about my mail."

Oh, yes, she would, but he'd save that for later. "We have plenty of other things to talk about."

"Please get down."

It hadn't escaped him that she couldn't leave until he did, since he blocked the exit to the plane. "First tell me why Viewmont's plane used to come in here only late at night, after hours?"

"What?" She twisted in her seat to get a good look at him, her eyes disbelieving. "What did you say?"

"Clark's plane," he said with mock patience, trying not to notice how deliciously rumpled she still looked. Her top button was only half done, beneath it her skin beckoned him. "It used to come in like clockwork every two weeks, at midnight, long after all the staff had left. Who helped him land?" He watched her wheels spin, and it was fascinating. "If it was all on the up-and-up, why not have the crew officially scheduled? What was he hiding? Illegal cargo?"

"Where did you learn that?" she whispered.

"Uh-uh. I asked you first."

Obviously pressed beyond endurance, she stood up and pushed at his thighs, desperate to get out. She couldn't get down—unless she wanted to crawl over him. He couldn't imagine she did. "What was he hiding, Sami?"

She shoved at him again, stubbornly mute. But he could be just as stubborn, especially over this. This involved Kevin, he just knew it, and for that he could wait all night.

"I'm not moving until you tell me." He sat firm.

She couldn't budge him, no matter how she tried. He crossed his arms over his chest and waited. A master negotiator, he knew when to push and when to retreat. She hesitated, then made her move, trying to climb over his legs, but only succeeded in getting herself hopelessly tangled up in them as he grabbed her waist and pulled her down on his lap.

"Tell me what's going on," he demanded as he wrestled with her, trying to restrain her. A flailing hand popped him hard under the chin, and he saw stars. "Stop it, Sami," he grated out as her knee nearly unmanned him.

"No." She grabbed the side of the plane and recklessly swung her leg over, nearly tumbling to the hard concrete below. Frantic, he grabbed her hips and pulled her back, his breath clogged in his throat. She was nuts. "You're going to fall, dammit!"

"Just let me go," she panted.

He couldn't. Wrapping his arms around her, he crushed her against him. Her legs slipped between his. Her bottom grounded into his crotch, and the intimacy of it all made it increasingly difficult to think. He could feel the frenzied beat of her heart. Her skirt had risen in their skirmish, and he feasted on the sight of her long, exposed length of thigh. She followed his gaze and with a sound of vexation, she yanked it back down, her elbow slamming into his stomach.

"Let go," she said in an uneven voice when he pulled her closer merely to protect himself. "Or I'll scream."

He released her immediately, sickened by the fear in her eyes. *She was afraid of him.* He quelled his temper, because while he was genuinely mad at her, he would never, *ever* hurt her.

She scrambled over him and down from the plane into the darkness below. He followed her, filled with self-disgust. He'd known, dammit he'd known, how a show of temper seemed to scare her. Hadn't he seen that in her office earlier?

She paused by the plane to smooth down her wrinkled clothes, her face hidden from him by the darkness.

"I didn't mean to scare you," he said quietly, standing next to her.

"Well then, stop doing it." She tucked her blouse back in with jerky movements that made him feel like a child molester.

How could he explain how critical this all was to him? "Where's your flashlight?"

"I don't know. It probably dropped in the plane."

Dillon tried to see down the black hallway and couldn't. He swore. "Wait here." She didn't answer, and he could well enough imagine the stubborn set of her chin, as well as her thoughts. "Sami?"

"Oh, for God's sake," she exploded. "I'll wait."

The only time he'd ever seen her remotely upset or unraveled was when she was dealing with him. It gave him little satisfaction that he seemed to bring out the worst in her. She did it to him as well. When he climbed down from the plane for the second time, she'd lost her fear and was armed with a question.

"How did you find out about Clark?"

Not surprise or shock. "I snooped into the files about the employee scheduling. I pulled the landings from Felicia's computer."

"You what—Why?"

Why indeed. "Let's just say I smelled a rat."

She did have a temper, he realized with some surprise. And he'd stirred it up something fierce. "Let's get something straight, Dillon Kinley." She jabbed at his chest with a neatly manicured nail. "I want you to stay away from me. And I want you to stay out of my affairs."

He caught her hand. "I guess that means you don't want to talk about it," he said grimly.

"Good guess." She yanked her hand back.

They walked the hall in silence, Sami wrapped in her own miserable thoughts. What had Clark and her father been up to? Why did it matter to Dillon?

He'd accused her of sleeping with Ricardo. He couldn't have been further from the truth, but she'd be damned if she was going to explain it after she'd humiliated herself in front of them both. It had been the day from hell. First her father had called to ask her to reconsider Clark's proposal. Clark himself had called her repeatedly. He'd made no specific threat, but somehow, she felt truly frightened of him.

She hated that—fear of a man. It made her feel like a young kid again, locked in a situation she had no control over. She'd thought she was completely free from that helpless, nightmare of a memory. Would it haunt her forever? She'd been eight years old when her mother, a rising stage actress, had fallen for her director.

And her director had had a thing against pretty, shy little girls. He'd made her life a living hell, punishing and tormenting when he could. Once her mother had realized what was happening, she'd been horrified, full of remorse and as spitting angry as she could be.

They'd never had another man in their house again. But for Sami, who'd never had a father, or even a brother or a true male friend, the damage had been done.

Men were not to be trusted.

Dillon's shoulder brushed hers, and she flinched back. He made a sound almost like regret, but that couldn't be, she realized. He thought of no one other than himself.

Finally, they reached the outside door.

Dillon grabbed her hand, and together they ran across the airstrip to the lobby. Without a word, she went directly to her office, grabbed her purse, and locked the door.

"Leaving?" he inquired sweetly from behind her.

She sighed and turned to face him. "Must you always follow me around?"

"I have one question, Sami."

"Leave me alone. *Please*."

"Why were you crying tonight, when I found you in the plane?"

She closed her eyes. "You caught me in a moment of weakness. It may surprise you to know, Dillon, that even I have emotions."

"It doesn't surprise me at all," he said in a low, intimate voice that had her stomach tightening. "I have another question."

"You said one."

"I lied. Are you sleeping with Ricardo?"

In his eyes was a burning desire to know, and a touching amount of uncertainty. "Do you really think I would kiss you the way I did if I was?"

He stared at her for a long minute, let out a deep,

shaky breath, and shoved his hands through his already messed-up hair. "Forget I asked."

It wasn't good enough. "You don't think very highly of me, Dillon, if you could ask that question in the first place."

"So the answer is no."

"The answer is no." She grasped her keys in fingers that wouldn't remain steady. She'd kissed this man who didn't trust her any more than she trusted him. She'd more than kissed him, she reminded herself. He'd touched her, and she'd nearly had a meltdown right there in his arms. God only knew what she would have done if Ricardo hadn't happened along, as humiliating as that had been. She knew her face flamed red. But his next words swiped the humiliation away.

"I want to know about those letters, Sami."

"They don't affect you."

Those light eyes narrowed, but he was careful to keep his distance. "Don't you want to see the report I told you about?"

"What I want is for you to stay away from me and anything that has to do with my business. Stop rifling through our computers and stop hitting up my employees for information, or you could be in violation of your lease."

He laughed shortly. "You'd like that, wouldn't you? You know what I think? I think you'd like to break our agreement so you'd be free to board Viewmont again. It's not going to happen, Sami. I have no intention of leaving, so get used to me."

He'd surprised her again. He'd known what Clark had wanted.

❖━━━━❖

Glancing back to make sure no one followed her, Sami slammed the door of hangar three. It was quite different in the light of day than it had appeared the night before, when she and Dillon had walked down the hall in ominous silence.

She hit the button of the cranky, ancient elevator, and it rose up to the second floor. She turned on lights, but they did nothing to dispel the dark, musty smell that assaulted her nostrils.

Her father kept her mother's things here, the things Debbie Reed had left behind when she'd deserted her husband twenty-five years before—but she wasn't looking to take a trip into the past.

Of the six offices, only one had been locked. She unlocked it and walked past the boxes of her mother's to the far corner of the shadowed room. A black duffel bag sat there alone. It had belonged to Kevin.

After his death, the authorities had attempted to contact his family. They'd discovered his parents were dead. He had a sibling that had been off in another part of the world and couldn't be reached. Sad as that was, Sami never knew what to do with his bag that had been in his locker in the maintenance hangar. She'd kept it, hoping one day she could give it to a relative.

She'd never looked through it, feeling as though that would be a great invasion of privacy. But now, after the letters she'd received and Dillon's suspicions that were quickly becoming her own, she felt she had to. She had to know if there was some sort of clue in it, something that would help her.

She dusted off the nearest chair and gingerly dragged the bag toward her.

At quitting time, Dillon made his way to Lucy's office. She frowned at the sight of him. The cute redhead had stopped giving him the time of day the minute she'd realized that Dillon and Sami had a basic mistrust of each other.

"You're back early," she said in an accusing tone.

"We had a nice tail wind."

"Hmm. Sami isn't in her office."

"Oh, that's all right." He gave her one of his most charming smiles—a smile that had gotten him what he'd wanted plenty of times. "I came to see you."

It was wasted on Lucy. He knew she was remembering the other day when he'd managed to finagle the information from her about Sami and Clark's meeting, and how Clark wanted his spot back. The one Kinley Charters currently occupied.

"I'm not going to tell you anything," she said primly, opening her drawer and sliding her pencil in.

Dillon's hand shot out and held the drawer open when she would have shut it. Slowly, since his blood had drained, he reached out and touched the small framed picture she had lying inside.

"That's Kevin," Lucy said. Her voice was quiet and filled with immeasurable sadness.

Dillon picked up the picture of his brother and held it close. Kevin grinned cheekily into the camera. . . . God, it hurt. "Where was this taken?"

"Here. Last year." Lucy reached up and touched

the photo in a way that had Dillon looking at her differently.

He had to clear his throat. "You were close."

She nodded. "I miss him very much."

Dillon knew right then and there, this woman was an ally. No one could watch her look at Kevin and think she'd had anything to do with his death.

He sighed, slipped the picture back into her drawer. His smile was softer, more gentle. "I'm sorry, Lucy."

Her phone rang, and she reached for it with a frown. "No, Sami's not in her office." She paused. "Mr. Viewmont, I've told you six times already. I'll tell her that you called." She dropped the phone on its cradle, looking disgusted.

"What does he want now?" Dillon asked.

Before she could answer, Felicia came toward them.

"Did you guys hear?" she asked breathlessly. "Mr. Reed might get out of the hospital next week."

"Poor Sami," said Lucy.

"Forget *her*," Felicia snorted delicately. "What about us? The man is a tyrant."

"You survived before," Dillon said, getting interested. A chance to meet Old Man Reed was good, real good. He glanced at Lucy's carefully blank face and knew. . . . Howard Reed would live up to his every expectation.

"Maybe that's why Sami disappeared," Lucy said.

"Disappeared?" Dillon repeated, getting *real* interested. Why would the picture of a loving daughter disappear at the news her father was coming unless . . . He didn't like his next thought.

If Howard Reed was the monstrous man he'd been led to believe, then how had he treated his daughter?

Had it been Reed who'd instilled that basic fear of men in her?

"Oh, she's just fine," Felicia said, exasperated.

But Lucy looked worried and unconvinced, and Dillon's unease grew.

It was only a hunch. And why Dillon cared, he didn't know. He couldn't say when it'd happened exactly, but he didn't like knowing he'd lied to Sami.

He wanted to tell her the truth.

But not until she came clean. She was hiding things. He shut the side door to hangar three quietly behind him. He'd brought his own flashlight this time, but the lights were on and he didn't have far to go. The elevator door swished open just as he passed them.

Sami stood in it, clutching a black duffel bag. She jumped when she saw him and put her hand on the elevator door, holding it open, but she didn't make a move to come out or to say anything. She just stood there, looking soft and wary. He might be the biggest idiot on earth, but he felt the most compelling urge to wrap his arms around her and never let go.

"Hi," he said inanely.

Her eyes narrowed, and she stepped back farther into the elevator, letting go of the door. It started to close, but he was quick enough to slap a hand against it, keeping it open. "You're still mad at me," he noted.

"Bingo."

"Come on. Really?"

She shook her head and let out a short, wry laugh. "Are you really so surprised? You've ridiculed me repeatedly, snooped into my private business affairs, and humiliated me in front of an employee." She looked at him. "Let go of the door."

"I've never ridiculed you," he insisted, still holding the door. "At least not intentionally. And you kissed me back," he pointed out, realizing his mistake when her chin came up sharply.

Her eyes shot daggers. *"Let go of the door!"*

"Okay." He stepped into the elevator and did as she'd asked, watching as the door closed with a loud screech.

Sami growled and slammed the open door button quickly.

He had no idea what got into him, but he hit the close door button, returning her high-handed look. The door slowly slid shut.

"Stop it!" She pushed him and smacked the open button. The door stopped its closing motion and hesitated briefly before opening again.

Dillon easily stepped around her and beat her to the panel, whacking the close button again. "Don't stop your plans on my account." He smiled amiably, enjoying her frustrated sigh.

The door closed and the elevator started to lift, noisily, when Sami pressed the open door button for the last time. He was just about to tease her for her stubbornness and apparent need to have the last word, when the elevator, its door still closed, crawled upward a few feet and jolted to a sharp stop.

Sami gained her balance and slapped the open button again. Nothing. She whirled on him, her brilliant eyes wide as saucers. "Now look what you've done. *We're stuck!"*

FIVE

"No. We're not stuck." Dillon calmly pressed the elevator open button. Nothing happened. He put the flashlight down and tried to pry the door open with his fingers.

"Great." Sami dropped her head back and stared at the ceiling as if waiting for divine intervention.

"This thing must be ancient," he said.

"It is!" She let out a muffled scream of frustration and slumped back against the wall of the elevator.

Used to move heavy parts from storage down to the hangar, the elevator hadn't been equipped with an emergency phone or panic button. "This sure wouldn't meet any required regulations," he remarked lightly.

"Well, sue me." She looked at him, steam practically coming out of her ears.

Like tears, a woman's temper had always been something he'd tried to avoid. Until Sami. For some sick reason, he enjoyed watching her go off. "I bet someone could. You should have a phone in here. And an alarm—"

She sighed loudly, closing her eyes.

He grinned. The irritation on her face was worth the entire trip.

"How are we going to get out?" she demanded.

He admired, reluctantly, what a good sport she was. "We're not—until someone finds us."

She just stared at him, squeezing that black bag close to her. She had that look about her again—the one that said she alone faced the world, and that it wasn't such a nice place. As usual, it did something to his insides. "You might as well relax," he suggested calmly, a little sorry he'd been goading her. "It might be a while."

The bag slipped to the floor with a thud. "It's going to be more than a while. No one knows where I am." She looked up at him hopefully. "Unless you told someone where you were going?"

He shook his head and forced the joviality out of his voice. No use upsetting her even more with the fact that he found this whole situation amusing. "No such luck."

"Why were you here anyway?"

"Looking for you," he admitted, turning away to try the door again.

"Whatever for?"

He gave up trying to pry the door open and leaned back against it. "Maybe I missed you."

She laughed, and he found himself staring at her in surprise. "I forgot you could do that."

She inhaled deeply.

"You have messages."

"I'm sure I do."

"Don't you want to know what they are?"

"No."

"Your father called," he said, watching for her reaction.

She sighed, loudly. "You were a trouble student, right?"

He could be just as stubborn. "What's he like?"

"We're stuck in an elevator, and you want to talk about my family?"

"Yeah." She wouldn't look at him. He lifted her chin with a finger. "What's he like, Sami?" He was unprepared for what the unhappiness and discontent in her eyes did to him.

"He's . . ." She shrugged. "I don't really know."

"What do you mean?"

"I don't really know him very well. He didn't raise me, and I never spent any time with him until recently." She stepped back. "And I don't know why I'm telling you this."

He slid his back down the wall until he sat on the floor. He held out a hand, but she shook her head with a wistful expression that he could only wonder at, shifting her weight on those long, gorgeous legs of hers. "What were you doing up there?" he asked curiously, nodding to the floor above them.

"Don't you ever get tired of bothering me?"

She was cute, he decided. Especially when annoyed. He grinned. "No."

"Oh, why can't you just be quiet and sit there?"

"I don't do the obedient thing so well. Used to drive my parents crazy. What were you doing up there?"

She gritted her teeth and studied the light above.

"It was just a polite question, Sami," he said evenly.

She closed her eyes. Being stuck in the elevator had brought on a touch of the vertigo that had plagued her since she'd been a child. She'd been uncomfortable in tight, high places since the day her mother's boyfriend—the dreaded director—had been baby-sitting her and she'd gotten locked, *supposedly* by accident, in her mother's dark, musty attic.

"I'm sorry," she whispered. "I just hate this."

He studied her quietly. "Being enclosed gets to you, doesn't it?"

She nodded, miserably embarrassed by the weakness he'd so easily detected.

"Claustrophobic?"

"A little." What was it about this man that he could draw her out when no one else could? "I'm fine."

She touched Kevin's bag with her toe. It had broken her heart to go through Kevin's things—a change of clothes, a pair of boots, a couple of stale candy bars, and the picture of Lucy and herself that Kevin had kept over his toolbox. The picture had been taken nearly a year before at a staff party Sami had attended, and Kevin had somehow ended up with it. He'd claimed he liked to see some inspiration for his work.

She glanced at Dillon, stretched out on the floor, looking as comfortable as if he'd been on a soft, plush couch. The man was a chameleon. And a damned attractive one. She had to get out of there, before she did something stupid. Like let him kiss her senseless again.

He yawned and stretched, and her eyes were caught by the quick flash of lazy, undulating pleasure that crossed his face. She'd seen that look once before—when he'd touched her. Her knees trembled.

"We might be here all night," he said casually.

"Oh my God."

"Sit down," he said calmly. "It's not all that bad."

She shook her head, envying Dillon's being able to plop down and sprawl on the floor. But it could never be done gracefully in the narrowly cut skirt she wore, and she refused to give him something else to enjoy.

"Come on, sit down." He patted the spot next to him invitingly, his eyes surprisingly open and friendly.

"Why are you being so nice?"

"I'm always nice." He ignored her scoff of disbelief. Then, after a minute, he said softly, "Please sit?"

"I can't," she admitted miserably, pulling at her tight skirt.

He looked at it curiously. To his credit, he didn't smirk or make fun of her. "Just hitch it up a little and kneel first," he suggested.

She searched his face for the tiniest sign of merriment, but there was none. She lifted her skirt a little to give her legs room to work. A strangled sound came from his side of the elevator, and she whipped her head toward him, but he was studying his tightly entwined hands in his lap.

When she sat, there was a long silence while he continued to watch his hands as if they held the utmost interest.

"Better?" he asked finally.

"Yes, thanks," she mumbled, resuming her own study of the ceiling. "How long is it going to take?"

"Maybe they've all left for the day."

She looked at him, horrified. "Would they?"

He shrugged. "I hope not, but you work late a lot. Maybe no one will think to come look for you."

The thought of being cooped up in this small space

for hours with Dillon was . . . well, disturbing to say the least. "You did."

His green eyes pierced through her, and she was struck by the genuine concern she read there. "I was worried about you."

His words broke the spell his gaze created. Finally, she could be amused at his expense. "Since when?"

He gave her a long look before he let his chin drop to his chest and stared at the floor. His hands were clasped loosely over his bent knees in a very masculine pose. After a long minute he said quietly, "We may be here a long time. Couldn't we try to get along?"

She looked at his strong, tanned hands and remembered how they'd pulled her to him the previous night and ran with amazing sensuous languor over her body. Of course, that had been before he'd assumed she'd slept with Ricardo and questioned her about Clark's dealings with Reed Aviation. "We *don't* get along," she reminded him. "It's no use trying."

"Funny," he said huskily, "I remember getting along fine with you last night."

"Before or after you called me a cheat?"

His smile faded. "I never called you a cheat."

"You accused me of trying to get rid of you so Clark could come back."

"Wasn't that the truth?" he asked quietly.

"No, it wasn't." Actually, what he'd told her about Clark bothered her very much. She couldn't think of one legal reason that Clark would need to come in regularly late at night without a staff on record.

"Your father called," he said. "He's getting out of the hospital."

"You seem to get a lot of information from Lucy

and Felicia. I thought I asked you to stop gossiping with my employees."

His eyes laughed at her. "I do not *gossip* and—"

"You do," she insisted, interrupting him. "And I want you to stop it."

"What I was going to say," he said patiently, "is that's not the point."

No, it wasn't. But she wasn't ready to face the point, so she looked away.

He'd been worried about her. What had Felicia told him?

They sat in silence. Every time Dillon moved, the leather of his bomber jacket rumpled together with a soft swishing sound that was strangely erotic. She remembered how that leather had felt under her own fingers when she'd held on to him.

The coolness of the concrete floor slowly seeped into her stocking-covered legs until every muscle felt stiff. She wished for her coat and eyed Dillon's longingly. *No.* She'd freeze to death before admitting she needed him or his jacket. He'd probably grin wickedly and offer to keep her warm. He'd run those incredibly warm, sure, and oh, so confident hands up and down her, and then—

"Cold?" he asked softly, nudging her with a shoulder.

"No." She shivered, and he laughed.

"Liar. Too bad you're so stubborn." He crossed his arms over himself and snuggled down. " 'Cause I'm really warm and toasty."

She glared at him.

"Sami, I'm kidding." He shrugged out of his jacket

and wrapped it around her shoulders, his hands lingering.

The jacket was indeed warm. So, all of a sudden, was the elevator. Their gazes met and held. He freed her hair from the collar, fingering it gently. "It's beautiful," he said in a low whisper.

She pulled the jacket close, knowing it'd been a mistake to accept it. It smelled like him, felt like him. Her breath caught at the yearning she saw in his eyes, and she had to swallow hard against the wave of unfamiliar desire rolling over her. She became very aware of their shoulders brushing against each other as they sat side by side, their hips touching, their legs connecting.

"Sami," he whispered roughly, plunging a hand into her hair at her nape. He reached over her and gently squeezed her hip, scooting even closer. Their lips nearly touched.

Then it happened.

Her stomach rumbled loudly in the small, silent elevator, echoing off the walls. Wanting to die from mortification, she slapped a hand over her tummy, leaned her head back, and closed her eyes.

It happened again, louder.

"Bellyache?" he inquired as if discussing body functions were an everyday topic. As if they were the best of friends. As if they were even on speaking terms!

It wasn't possible to be more embarrassed. "No. It's nothing."

He drew back slightly to see her face, his hand still caressing her hip. "It's *something*," he insisted.

Did he ever give up? She opened her eyes. "I'm hungry, okay?" She hadn't eaten since breakfast. She snuggled in deeper to the heavy warmth of Dillon's jacket and looked anywhere but at him.

Dillon stared at his jacket, then at her. His gaze held a strangely soft gleam, as if he liked the picture of her in his clothes. She shifted her weight away from him, disturbed by the way her body had reacted.

"I'm hungry too," he said finally. He sat upright and nodded to the black bag hopefully. "Don't women always have something to eat in their purse?"

"It's a myth. Besides, it isn't my purse."

"What is it then?"

"It's—" She stopped short, not sure what to say.

"It's what?"

She didn't feel up to explaining the bag. It seemed ghoulish of her to have even opened it. But then she remembered the candy bars. "I couldn't."

"Couldn't what?"

Had she said that out loud? She clutched the bag protectively to her chest. "Don't take it."

"Sami, you aren't making much sense."

"I thought you were going to take it."

He ran an impatient hand across his forehead. "You're unbelievable, you know that? I may be a lot of things, but I sure as hell am *not* a purse snatcher." She just stared at him, and he made a sound of disgust. "Give me some credit."

"It's got candy bars in it," she said softly. "Two of them. They're old, probably stale, but it's all we've got. Want one?" She opened the zipper and pulled out the candy bars.

But his gaze was riveted on the contents of the bag, fully exposed by the opening. He gripped her wrist.

"Where did you get that shirt?" His voice sounded as if he'd forced it past severely damaged vocal cords.

The shirt did look unusual, but she recognized it immediately. Kevin had worn it under his mechanic's overalls. It was a long-sleeved T-shirt that had a unique white hand-painted logo on the front.

"This isn't yours. Where did you get it?" he demanded, tugging on her wrist until she looked at him.

She gave serious consideration to lying, but decided against it. He'd obviously seen one like it and would know if she didn't tell the truth. "It's—Hey."

He dropped her arm and grabbed the bag, spilling out the contents across the small concrete floor. Her heart tipped a little at the sight of Kevin's belongings scattered at her feet. Dillon's lips drew tightly together in a harsh line. He exhaled sharply as he touched each item from the bag. "Work boots, pants . . . these things aren't yours." Then he saw the picture of her and Lucy. His eyes, cold as daggers of ice, lifted to hers. "This isn't your purse."

"I told you it wasn't."

He ran his hands over the few meager possessions, collecting them possessively off the floor and cradling them in his lap. Confusion filled Sami at the contrast of his cruel voice to his almost caressing hands as they handled the red shirt.

"Why do you have his things?" His voice was so hushed, she could hardly hear him.

She gaped at him, but a sound pierced through her jumbled senses. Someone was calling her name.

She stood up abruptly and collided with Dillon as he did the same. She backed herself against the wall as he followed her. Her head tilted back, and her eyes locked with his cold, furious ones.

"Tell me," he pressed.

"Sami . . . ," a far off voice called.

"*Tell me!*" Dillon grated.

"Stop it!" Gut-wrenching fear gripped her as her vertigo kicked in. Dizziness made her head swim, and for a second, she was back, locked in her mother's attic, a terror-filled child. "They're looking for us." She pushed hard with her hands against his chest, and he moved away so suddenly, she nearly fell back against the elevator door. She whirled and pounded with two fists on the closed door, screaming, "In here! We're in the elevator."

"Sami," Dillon said tersely behind her. "We need to talk. The bag and the letters. They're—"

"Can you hear me?" she called out, ignoring him. Her heart pounded. She hit the door as hard as she could.

"Hold on," Ricardo's voice called back. "We'll get you out. But it's going to take a minute."

"Sami," Dillon said in a low voice. "Look at me."

She couldn't. She could barely breathe.

"I'm sorry," he said, touching her arm, but she flung him off. "I didn't mean to scare you, but I've got to know."

"You keep saying that," she said shakily, putting her palms and forehead on the door, feeling Ricardo's efforts on the other side. "You don't mean to scare me. But you keep doing it."

"I would never hurt you, you've got to know that." The wounded tone was real, so was the regret, and she wanted to believe him, but old habits were difficult to break. "Go away, Dillon."

"I can't." Gently, easily, he turned her around to face him. "We're locked in an elevator together, remember?" Emotion still boiled in his eyes, in his rigid stance. But his touch remained light. "You shocked me, Sami. To the core. What's going on?"

"I need to know the same thing," she whispered, leaning against the wall as far away from him as she could. Her fear had subsided, but she still wanted no contact. "You're keeping secrets."

They stared at each other in an almost unbearable silence, then suddenly the door was pried open, revealing a worried-looking Ricardo and Jim. Sami had never felt such relief.

"What happened?" Ricardo asked, looking back and forth between a stubbornly silent Dillon and a mortified Sami.

"Never mind," she hastened to say, brushing into the hallway, taking a deep breath. She felt as if she'd been freed from life imprisonment. "How did you find us?"

"Lucy made us search," Ricardo said in a carefully neutral voice.

Sami glanced at Dillon. He was staring at her, his face a mask of granite. A shudder rippled through her at the thought of spending the night alone with him, locked in that small, cramped elevator; although she had to be honest and admit—she didn't trust herself any more than she trusted him.

She slipped out of his jacket and handed it to him. He took it wordlessly. "Thank you," she said coolly.

He just turned away.

Not until an hour later when she lay soaking in a hot tub did Sami realize she'd forgotten Kevin's bag. Dripping wet, she dashed to the phone to call Jim and Ricardo. Neither of them had seen it. Which meant one thing.

Dillon had the bag. And he'd known Kevin well enough to recognize an item of clothing.

What would an out-of-town charter pilot—one who claimed to have never before been in Bear Pass—know about a private airport mechanic who'd died?

A week later, Sami slammed the phone down. Clark's secretary wanted her to know Clark would land in a matter of minutes, and he expected fuel and a mechanic standing by for his convenience.

She'd see about that.

She threw on her coat and marched out of the lobby into the brisk autumn day. The crisp air filled her lungs, and she took in the gorgeous mountain peaks of Bear Pass. Crossing the airstrip, she entered the maintenance hangar.

"Sami." Ricardo turned his head toward her quickly, his dark eyes completely unmasked as he so rarely allowed them to be. They were filled with a surprising hot ache. For her. She froze . . . and forgot what she was going to say. Then he blinked, and the old Ricardo was back. She backed up and gave him a shaky smile.

The large man came to his feet. "What's up?"

He didn't know what he'd shown her, thank God.

"How busy are you today?" she asked, striving to be normal.

"We've got four planes to be serviced and only three mechanics."

"Viewmont's coming through. If he needs to be serviced, place him in line."

"He'll insist."

"Don't give in." She left as quickly as she could.

Once outside again, between hangars, she paused to pull her long coat tighter around her and to take a deep breath. She hated knowing Ricardo hurt over her, but she couldn't give him what he wanted. She didn't feel the same way.

At the drone of an incoming plane, she hastened her step, knowing it would be Clark. But the plane came into sight before she could dash across the other airstrip to the safety of her office. She slipped into the offices she'd rented to Dillon, correctly assuming he'd be out on a flight. They'd hardly spoken since the elevator fiasco. He'd been flying every day, and she'd made an effort to be gone by the time he came in for the night.

She sank into his chair, peeling off her coat. The isolation appealed to her. Here, far from the lobby and across an empty hangar, she wouldn't be disturbed. Dillon had even closed the shutters on both windows.

"Deep in thought?" Clark stood in the doorway.

"Very," she said in her strongest leave-me-alone-and-go-away voice.

"Change offices?" He walked slowly into the room, looking every bit the suave businessman in an Armani suit with his dark hair combed smoothly back from his face.

"No." She willed him to go away, but he leaned neatly manicured hands on Dillon's desk, his heavy cologne prevailing her senses until she felt suffocated.

"You've been ignoring me, Sami. You haven't returned my calls."

"I've been busy."

He glanced around, apparently noting the lack of work in front of her and the relaxed pose she'd been in when he'd entered the room. His black eyebrows rose. "Oh, I can see that."

"What do you want, Clark?"

"A mechanic."

"They're busy. We'll get you one as soon as we can."

"I had my secretary call in ahead." He shook his head and gently chided, "This isn't the agreement I had here in the past. I thought your father would have made that clear to you by now."

"My father is no longer running Reed Aviation. I am."

His smile disappeared. "I was told you'd reconsidered my proposal." His voice had lost its pleasant note.

She leaned back in Dillon's chair. "You heard wrong. But you're welcome to come through here, just like any other customer. Any *paying* customer."

"I think," he said softly, moving around to the side of Dillon's desk and leaning against it, "you'll reconsider."

She didn't know exactly what Clark wanted from her. He was rich, more than rich. Saving a few dollars here or there couldn't possibly matter to him. There had to be something else. He seemed to want the run of the place, the freedom to come and go as he pleased, but for what, she could only guess. "Did you know that I've hired two additional line crew? There's now someone here to receive incoming planes twenty-four hours a day," she lied smoothly.

He carefully masked his quick flash of surprise. "Why?"

"I discovered we had quite a need for it in the past. After all, you alone came in after hours many, many times."

Another flash of emotion in his dark eyes, this time anger. She became inexplicably nervous and stood up abruptly, unable to stand feeling penned in by him a second longer.

"Leave it alone, Sami."

She didn't like the menacing tone or the fact she suddenly felt so uncomfortable in his presence. She was alone in an isolated office far from the lobby, and the shades were shut. So was the door, she noted with rising panic. No one could see them, and definitely no one could hear them.

He took a step closer, trapping her between the desk, Dillon's chair, and himself. "Your father made me very welcome here, and he made it clear you would do the same." He smiled coldly, their eyes on the same level. "I remember when I first saw you, Sami." He picked up a strand of her hair and twisted it in his fingers. "I thought you were soft and beautiful. I looked forward to dealing with you instead of your father."

She slapped his hand away, her heart in her throat. She wouldn't let him scare her, but her pulse raced regardless. "What were you doing on those late night flights?"

"Business."

She tried to back up, but the chair firmly blocked her path. She gripped the edge of the desk, and her fingers fell on something cold and sharp. The letter opener. Behind her back, she clenched it in her hand. He touched her shoulder, rubbing the silk of her blouse. "Was your father right, Sami? Are you going to make me welcome here?"

She couldn't stand the closeness, could hardly breathe. She tried to push past him, but he blocked her. Unless she wanted to touch him, which she most certainly did not, she couldn't get past him. "What's the rush? You didn't answer me."

His tone sounded disgustingly pleasant, but his eyes remained stone-cold. She became very afraid. The weight of the letter opener didn't help. "I told you under what terms you were welcome here."

Her balance was precarious, leaning away from him as she was, and trapped with the chair pressing against the back of her knees. She glanced longingly at the just-out-of-reach phone.

"You don't really want me to leave, do you?" His soft voice sent shivers down her spine. "Think of how upset your father will be. Why, it might even *kill* him. Come on, Sami. Let's come to some arrangement." He reached for her then, with his soft, hot hands, but she shrank back, nearly falling over the chair.

"I want you to leave. Now," she nearly screamed, finally losing her balance and unceremoniously toppling over into Dillon's chair, nearly stabbing herself with the letter opener.

He quickly grabbed the armrests and leaned in, smiling wickedly. "I don't think so. Not just yet."

SIX

Sami lifted the letter opener in shaky hands. "Leave," she repeated. Clark looked at the "weapon" and laughed.

"She said 'leave,' Viewmont. Something wrong with your hearing?" Dillon leaned solidly in the doorway, his eyes cold, expression unreadable.

Sami sagged in relief.

But Clark didn't move, didn't take his gaze from Sami. "Stay out of it."

"Get out," Dillon said in a deceptively soft voice. His lounging position looked casual enough, but Sami knew better. Every muscle in that body was coiled tight, and given his icy features, he was more than up for a fight.

"Go taxi someone somewhere," Clark tossed over his shoulder.

Dillon's jaw tightened at the thinly veiled insult. "You have two seconds to get out of my office." He pushed away from the doorway and moved toward them. "Make that one." He shrugged out of his jacket and tossed his sunglasses down on his desk. Clark quickly straightened, but made no move to leave. He still blocked Sami. "Have it your way," Dillon said, moving toward Clark.

Sami struggled clumsily to an upright position in the chair, hoping to avoid a nasty confrontation. She spoke urgently to Clark, keeping an eye on the dangerously quiet Dillon. "Just go. I don't want any trouble."

"Call off your watchdog, Sami. We can finish this in your office."

"No," Dillon said through clenched teeth.

"We're not through," Clark said to Sami, moving purposefully to the door. "Not by a long shot."

When he finally left, Sami took a deep breath of air, waiting for her pounding heart to settle. She stood on shaky limbs and turned with a sheepish smile to Dillon, intending to thank him for his very timely arrival.

Her smile froze. He stood next to his desk, his sleeves pushed up to his biceps. A tight scowl covered his face. He had the look of a man who'd been spoiling for a fight, only to find his opponent already down for the count.

"I'd appreciate it if you'd have your little lovers' spats in your own office," he announced without even glancing at her. He dropped himself down into the chair she'd just vacated and pulled his unopened mail toward him. He held out his hand. "If you're not going to stab anyone with that, I could use it here."

It took her a second to realize he meant the letter opener. Swallowing hysterical laughter, she dropped it on his desk, listening to the clatter of steel on wood.

He proceeded to work as if she wasn't standing right there. First he'd accused her of having a fling with

Ricardo, and now, of all people, Clark. It was simply too much. She opened her mouth to announce him wrong, but then shut it again. To do so, she'd have to admit the situation had gotten out of hand and that she'd needed his help—which was the last thing she wanted to do. But, dammit, her shaky legs wouldn't take her out where she could collapse in privacy.

A minute later, when she still hadn't moved, he lifted his head and asked in an overly polite voice, "Was there something you needed?"

Yes, she wanted to cry, still in shock over Clark's strangely terrifying behavior, *there is something I need. I want to be held, I want to be told I'm all right . . . I want a hug.*

Dillon sent her a stony look before averting his gaze back to his mail, but all he could see was Viewmont hanging all over her. He wanted to be furious with her. He certainly had plenty of reasons, not the least being that she continually disrupted his life with just a blink of those incredible eyes. Okay, he was soused in jealousy and he knew it. And what made it all the more disgusting was that it wasn't even her fault.

He couldn't maintain his anger. She stood there, staring at him uncertainly, fearfully, and he wanted to go smash Viewmont's face in. His blood ran cold when he thought about what could have happened if he hadn't come back when he did.

"You okay?" he asked finally, gruffly.

She let out a short laugh.

"Why do you put up with that?"

She raised her chin. "It's—"

"—none of my business," he finished for her. He

turned and shoved a file back into the file cabinet behind his desk. "It should be someone's concern."

"I can handle myself."

"Oh, yeah," he said with a sneer, yanking out several files that he had no idea if he needed. "And you're doing a great job of it too. You've got a father who could care less about you, a head mechanic whose loyalties are not your own, and a customer who gets his kicks from being a bully."

"You don't know my father."

"That's right," he agreed, slapping the files to his desk. "I don't. And what I hear, I should be grateful for that."

"What do you mean about Ricardo?"

"Just what I said."

"Ricardo would never hurt me or Reed Aviation."

"Whatever." He gave her a long stare, wondering why he cared. "At least tell me why the hell you put up with Viewmont. What would have happened if I hadn't come back early today?" His stomach clenched at the thought.

"I would have been fine."

"Yeah. Because you had my letter opener." His gut twisted again. "Would you have been able to use it?" Her face answered for him, and he shook his head. "Why, Sami?" he pushed. "Why do you put up with it?"

Her hazel eyes flashed wildly as her temper stirred. It was fascinating to watch. "Stay out of my affairs and my life!"

"Fine. Gladly." They stared at each other until Sami was paged over the intercom. She stormed to Dillon's desk.

"Problem?" he asked when she hung up the phone with a frown.

She headed for the door, her heels clicking louder than he'd heard yet. "Mechanics are overloaded."

She'd gotten to the hangar's outside door when she glanced at him in surprise. "What are you doing?"

"Maybe I can help."

She walked out ahead of him, squinting in the bright afternoon sunlight. "There's not much you can do unless you wield a wrench as well as you can pilot a plane."

Few could and Dillon knew it. "I can."

"Why?"

"I learned a long time ago—"

She made a face as they walked, and waved her hand. "Not that. I meant, why are you helping me?"

"Can't someone do something for you without having an ulterior motive?"

"Not you, I don't think."

"Shame on you." At least her color had returned, even if it was from anger. "You don't know me well enough to judge me."

She gave him an indecipherable look. At Ricardo's office, he paused to hold open the door for her, but she faltered briefly when she saw Clark seated in a chair. Dillon pushed her gently in, very glad he'd accommodated her.

"Ricardo. How's it going?"

They'd never know how upset and terrified she'd looked a few minutes ago, Dillon thought, his admiration growing.

"We're swamped," Ricardo said.

"Yeah, we can see how busy you are," Dillon said dryly.

Clark flushed angrily. "Do you have a solution, Kinley? Or are you going to stand there and waste more time?"

"Actually," he said, looking at Ricardo. "I came to offer help. Want it?"

"You bet we want it. Let's go."

"I want my plane ready today," Clark said.

Ricardo looked at Sami. "Absolutely not," she said. "Take them in line."

"This is ridiculous," Clark stated. "Will I be charged for housing the plane overnight?"

"Of course not."

Clark snorted as he strode furiously to the door and then slammed it behind him. Ricardo watched him go and sighed heavily.

"Don't worry about it," Sami told him.

"Don't worry about it?" he repeated, shaking his head. "Your father is going to have my hide for this. It's a good thing I didn't burn any bridges at Mountain Aircraft." He nodded curtly to Dillon. "Let's go."

Dillon stood near the far wall of the lobby, staring up at the aviation maps spread across the wall. He'd been standing there some time, alone.

Felicia came in. She shut off the lights, unplugged the coffee pots, and moved around locking doors, stopping when she saw him. "Oh, you startled me." She came up to him, standing much closer than necessary, and smiled. "What are you still doing here?"

"Just looking." There were various pins stuck into

the map, most of them red, some yellow. "What are the pins for?"

"It's an old ritual here. Pilots stick the red pins on their favorite spots in the sky. The yellow ones are from people who work here."

Dillon pointed to the one black pin, indicating a location not too many miles north of where they were. "What's this one for?"

Felicia's pretty smile turned upside down. "That one marks where Kevin died."

He tensed. His mouth went dry. "What happened?"

"It was Ricardo's birthday, and we were having cake and ice cream in the hangar. Clark's plane had been in for two days getting certain repairs." She gave him a wry smile. "He insisted on having his plane tested right then and there."

"In the middle of a party?"

She nodded, for once looking suitably subdued. "Everyone was relaxed from the party. No one wanted to test the plane. Ricardo thought it should wait until morning, but Clark insisted."

"So why Kevin?"

"Besides Ricardo, who'd already had a drink and couldn't fly, Kevin was the only other mechanic that was a pilot."

"Had Kevin flown Clark's plane before?"

"Many times. They were always making him fly that thing, even when he didn't want to."

He hated the image that projected, his brother being forced into something he hadn't wanted. And now he was dead. The guilt washed over him. "*They?* As in who?"

"Mr. Reed or Clark."

"That's strange," he said, feeling cold down to his bones. "A pilot usually lives to fly."

"Dillon," she purred softly, "the only thing that seems strange is why you aren't responding to me." She pressed her body to his. Her dark eyes had a shine of promise in them that he couldn't mistake. For an instant, just an instant, he considered it—as a means to shake this sudden desperate hopelessness in him. *God, Kevin,* he thought, *I'm so sorry. So damned sorry.*

Felicia wrapped her long arms around his neck and pulled his head down, running a wet tongue along his ear. He closed his eyes and tried to make himself feel something, *anything,* but he didn't. *Couldn't.* Her hair wasn't a golden shimmering halo. Her eyes weren't wide, hazel ones, filled with emotion. Wrong woman, he thought dismally, lifting his hands to set her away from him.

"Oh!" The soft exclamation was accompanied by a thud, as Sami dropped her briefcase.

"Sami?" Felicia squinted in the darkness.

She couldn't speak, not yet. She'd come into the darkened lobby on her way out for the night, just as the two shadows entwined against the wall had moved apart. And her heart had slipped quietly to the floor.

She bent to retrieve her briefcase. Anger was good, she told herself, it pushed back the strange sense of betrayal. "I'm sure our customers would appreciate it if in the future, you'd take it somewhere else. Like a hotel room," she added, proceeding through the lobby as if nothing had happened. So why was she suddenly fighting tears?

She paused at the front door to set down her work

and button her coat. It was, of course, pouring. To her surprise, her hands weren't quite steady. Dillon could kiss whomever he wanted, she reminded herself. Yet, she had trouble with that last button, then had to fumble through her purse searching for her keys.

"Need help?" that annoyingly familiar voice asked behind her.

"No." She shook her purse. No keys. She threw the purse down and picked up her briefcase, rifling through that too.

"I don't think I've ever seen you quite so ruffled before," he remarked mildly, watching her with laughing eyes.

"I am *not* ruffled." So why the hell couldn't she find her keys?

"Really?"

"*Really.*" She tossed down her briefcase in disgust and ran flustered hands through her pockets. Empty.

"Then what's missing?" He smiled at her innocently.

Damn him, but he was enjoying this. She sighed audibly. "Keys, if you must know. I can't find my keys."

Felicia came through, a discreet smile playing about her lips. "Good night."

To Sami's unending exasperation, Dillon returned the smile. "Thanks. Drive safe."

Sami watched Felicia glance at Dillon as though she wanted to eat him alive, and she gritted her teeth together, locked in the memory of them wrapped around each other in the lobby, embracing.

Dillon laughed softly. *At her.* Since she wouldn't be lucky enough to have the ground swallow her up whole, she stared at him defiantly, daring him to say something.

"Did you check your office?"

"What?"

His eyes still reflected his amusement. "Your keys," he reminded her patiently. "Did you check your office for them?"

They walked back together, with Sami protesting all the way that she could find them without his help. "What if you don't?" he argued. "You'll be stranded here by yourself."

While being alone seemed infinitely preferable to her alternative, she didn't see that she had much choice. Her spare set *was* at home. She'd need a ride. "Fine."

He raised his eyebrows, giving her that innocent look again. As if he'd *ever* been innocent. "What are you so mad at?"

He'd touched Felicia. Sami had let him do the same to her. Oh, she was plenty mad—at herself. "I've asked you not to sit around and waste my employees' time. They're busy."

A knowing smile played about his lips. "Things are not always as they seem, Sami. You should know that."

"Were you or were you not kissing Felicia just now?"

"Would that bother you?"

"Not in the least," she lied. They came to her office door, which was locked tight.

"Don't you have an extra set?"

"Yes." She was getting more provoked by the passing second. She took a deep breath, trying the relaxation method that had failed her ever since Dillon Kinley had come to Bear Pass. "At home." She could see his eyes flashing with humor and how he struggled not to laugh. "It's not really all that funny."

"Are you *kidding?*" he asked, giving up and grinning broadly. "The totally together Ms. Reed losing her composure *and* her keys?"

She tried to not be affected by his smile. She'd known, *she'd known* that smile would be trouble from that very first day.

They walked in silence down the dark hallway. "What did you mean when you said things aren't always as they seem?"

He was quiet for a long moment, and Sami got the impression he picked his words carefully as he turned to her. "Today I walked into my office and found you and Clark in what looked like a compromising situation. You could have been lovers having a little spat." He paused meaningfully. "But that's not even close to what really happened, is it?"

She stared at him, her eyes huge. "No," she whispered, feeling foolish, and a little overcome by the sudden compassion and warmth in his eyes. The horror of the near catastrophe faded quickly under his understanding gaze. And for some reason, she pushed on, knowing there was more. "What else? What else isn't as it seems?"

He watched her quietly. "Kevin's accident." Without another word, he turned and walked down the hall.

When he helped her out of the rain and into his Jeep a few minutes later, his face was clean of expression. She directed him which way to go and then the conversation lagged. The rain continued to come down, hitting the car with a soothing rhythm.

"Busy day," Dillon said after a few long minutes. "The maintenance department's hopping."

"Thankfully."

"Did you ever hire a replacement for Kevin?"

She turned her head toward him. "Why? Need a job?"

"Do you *ever* answer a question?"

"No, I didn't hire a replacement. At the time, there wasn't a need to."

"And now?"

"Now it looks like maybe I should. Turn right."

The rain hadn't slowed, but he handled the Jeep in the slippery weather like a pro. The way he handled everything. "Do any of your mechanics fly?"

"Not anymore. Are you ever going to tell me, what is this preoccupation you have with my business?"

"Maybe. Someday."

He got off the highway when she indicated, and she found herself studying his strong hands sliding over the steering wheel. Then came the unbidden memory of how those hands had slid over her. She had to take a deep breath.

"So why don't any of your mechanics fly?"

If his hands had mesmerized her, his eyes positively hypnotized her. They compelled, urged, searched for something she didn't understand. "It's rare to find a gifted airplane mechanic who can also fly a variety of aircraft."

"Who tests the planes after you've done major renovations or maintenance?"

"The owner of the plane or his pilot. Our mechanic accompanies him."

"Does Viewmont fly his own plane?"

"He can," she answered cautiously. "But he usually has his pilot fly him."

He pulled up to the gate of her condominium complex. The rain came down in droves, slamming down onto the top of the Jeep with a loud roar that echoed eerily inside. Dillon's windshield wipers were on high, and they squeaked noisily, sloshing water off the sides.

He let the Jeep idle. "So mostly his pilot flies for him?" he pushed.

"That's what Clark prefers."

His eyes narrowed, and in the darkened interior the shadows from the headlights highlighted off the planes of his face. He looked more dangerous than ever. "Then why did his plane go down with one of your employees on board, piloting by himself?"

She stared at him, filled with trepidation. She hadn't wondered about it, *until the mysterious letters*. Now she thought of little else. "Maybe Clark's pilot had been unavailable. It happens."

"Doesn't that seem strange to you?"

"Yes," she whispered.

His fingers tightened on the headrest above her head and the stick shift between them until his knuckles whitened. "Then why haven't you done anything about it?"

The unfairness of that hit her hard. She'd just started to question the events of that fateful day. The FAA had closed the case. "What would you have me do? The reports said the fire was caused by faulty wires." There'd been nothing left, everything burned to a crisp. They hadn't even been able to recover

Kevin's body. She shuddered at what he must have gone through in his final moments.

Dillon looked at her with mild censure. "In other words, they don't know what the hell happened."

"They never proved any wrongdoing, as you seem to suspect," she said defensively. "I don't understand, Dillon. *What does this have to do with you?*"

He reached for her security card and slid it through, waiting in silence until the gates slowly opened in front of them. "And you think *I* don't answer questions well," she muttered.

If she wanted to continue to run this business, she needed to get to the bottom of this whole mess. She needed to face her father and his past. She needed to confront Clark and whatever it was he'd threatened her with. She needed to resolve the issue of Kevin's death. But mostly, she needed to learn what Dillon Kinley was about.

Not a small order.

Dillon turned into her driveway. The fog had rolled in so low that the headlights disappeared into it, vanishing within inches of the front of the car.

"I bet the airport is socked in tonight," he said, turning off the Jeep.

"What are you doing?"

"I'm walking you in."

She shrugged, suddenly too weary to argue. They had to run through the drenching rain around the corner of the condo to the front door, since her garage door opener was locked inside her car at the airport. The wind assaulted them, too, so that by the time they got to her porch, they were soaked to the bone.

With a surreptitious glance at Dillon, Sami pulled her hidden key out of a flowerpot.

"You've got to be kidding me," he said with a sharp shake of his wet head. "Can't you find a better place to hide that thing?"

"Lucky for me it is here," she said haughtily. "Or I'd have been really stuck."

"Hmmm." He thought about that and lifted his eyebrows. "You would have been at my mercy."

She didn't like that gleam in his eyes. "I'd have figured it out."

"That's right," he said lightly. "Because you're fine and it's none of my business."

She stiffened, then realized he was teasing her.

"You'd have figured it out all right," he said in a suddenly sobered voice. "Even if it meant sleeping in the cold lobby rather than asking for my help."

She unlocked the door, wondering why that had left her so confused and unsure. "It's a long drive back to the airport." She knew he was as cold and wet as she was because he'd shoved his hands in his pockets and shifted his weight back and forth on his feet, trying to keep moving. She watched in riveted fascination at the water running in little rivulets down his chiseled features. "Do you want to come in and see if you can wait out the worst of this storm?"

He hesitated, and she nearly told him to forget it. She'd been crazy even to consider inviting this strange, moody man into her home. He badgered her at every opportunity, was short-tempered, abrupt, and couldn't stay out of her personal affairs to save his life. But he was also marvelously intuitive. A mechanical genius.

Compassionate. And she couldn't forget wildly attractive. He'd kissed her with an unbridled passion, that until he'd shown her, she'd never would have believed.

"Yes," he said quietly, startling her from her thoughts. "I'll come in."

SEVEN

Sami's condo surprised Dillon. The furniture in the living room was sparse: a small forest-green couch, an oak coffee table, a comfortable-looking plaid chair. But the walls really caught his attention. There were pictures of airplanes everywhere. He turned to her, surprised and delighted.

"It's kind of a hobby." She shrugged shyly and slipped off her wet coat. She streaked her wet hair off her face and gave him a little smile.

"Why didn't you tell me?" He slipped out of his jacket and hung it on the door handle.

"When?"

"I guess we haven't done much idle chatting, have we?" He knew a real flash of regret that they always seemed to be on opposite sides of the fence. But all he wanted was the truth. Yet, he hadn't been exactly honest either.

"Tea?" she asked from the doorway to the kitchen. "Or does a man like you need something stronger?"

Her expression was so perfectly bland, he had no

idea if she was teasing him or not. Then her eyes flared, daring him. He grinned. "You've got a little ruthless streak, don't you?"

One corner of her mouth quirked up. "Isn't it funny how we always recognize our own qualities in others?"

"Ouch." He lifted a brow. "You've got mascara running down your face."

"Add heartless to your list." She swiped under her eye and inspected her hand. "I do not."

He laughed. "Yes, you do. And I do so have a heart." He rubbed a hand over it. It ached every time he looked at her. "And you're breaking it right now," he told her, startled to realize he was only half kidding.

"Right." She gave him a look of amused derision. "Have you ever actually had your heart broken?"

"Twice."

"Twice? That unpenetrable, solid-stone excuse for an organ has been broken twice?"

He grinned again. "Shelly Martin. She crushed me."

"Oh." She turned away.

"I was in the first grade," he said, enjoying himself when she sent him a vintage Sami Reed look.

"And the second time?"

The day I met you, he almost said, then stopped short. He blinked, for a minute completely stunned. "Awfully curious about someone you don't like much, aren't you?"

Her smile faded. "Tea?"

"Sounds good." He wandered from picture to picture while she went into the kitchen. "That plane you were in the other night," he called to her. "Is it yours?"

"Sort of." He heard the water run. "It's my mother's."

"Is it for sale?"

A pot banged onto the stove. "No. It's old and needs lots of work, but I couldn't part with it."

"It's a gem," he agreed. "But it's just rotting where it is. Do you suppose if I made her an offer, she'd consider it?"

The cluttering in the kitchen stopped abruptly. "It's not getting any worse where it is."

"It's just a shame to see a wonderful old plane like that go to waste. Why doesn't she fix it up?"

Sami appeared in the doorway, wearing a somber, almost haunting expression. "She's dead."

He could see the deep pain in her eyes. He recognized it well because he dealt with the same sort of pain every day and sharing it with her set off a fierce protectiveness toward her that he couldn't explain. "I'm sorry," he said, very aware of the inadequacy of those words.

"Tea's ready."

He couldn't seem to satisfy his curiosity about her. Over his second cup of tea he learned she loved to fly, but her vertigo had prevented her from being a pilot. "Didn't your father ever take you flying?"

She gripped her cup tightly and stared down into her cooling tea. "No."

"I'd take you."

Her face lit up with such enthusiasm that he wondered how long it had been since someone had offered to do something for her.

"Do you think—Oh, never mind."

"What?" he pushed, having felt so intoxicated by

the brightness of her smile, he'd promise her the moon to get it back.

"I was thinking of my mother's plane. I'd love to take it up sometime."

"It flies?"

"Oh, yes," she breathed with such hope that he knew he'd fly it even if he killed himself trying. "It only needs cosmetic things. But if you don't think you can . . ."

He grinned at the challenge. He could have told her there wasn't a plane out there he couldn't fly, but he'd show her. "Just tell me when."

"It needs to be checked out. I'll ask Ricardo."

"I'll do it."

She cocked her head, her eyes still shining luminously. "You are a man of all trades, aren't you?"

"I guess I am."

A picture on the wall drew him. A little girl held on tightly to a woman's hand in front of a crop duster biplane. He recognized the plane immediately as the one they'd been talking about.

"Yes, it's me," she said softly. "And my mother."

The sudden huskiness of her voice told him how much the picture meant to her. She stood there in pigtails and overalls, wearing such a serious, intent look on her little face that his heart ached for her. Her mother was incredible looking, and Sami was the spitting image of her now. He put a hand on the small desk beneath it to lean closer, but stopped when his fingers touched a bare photograph. He glanced down and went completely still. Shock seeped into his bones, freezing him in place.

Above his fingers were the letters about Kevin. Beneath them were three pictures of a horrific plane accident. With a hard, sinking feeling deep in his belly, he knew what he stared at was Kevin's accident. Bile rose. The first photo showed an overview of the plane, completely charred with nothing but a bare frame left. His hand shook violently as he lifted it to study the second. It showed the interior, or more correctly, burned metal. The third was a close-up of what would have been the cockpit. The only reason he recognized it as such was because of the shape of the nose of the plane. His brother had died in this. He swallowed hard and wished desperately for something to throw.

Still referring to her mother's plane, Sami quipped, "That was when the plane was in good shape."

Kevin had been *in* that charred disaster. His throat burned. So did the back of his eyes. His good mood had shattered, he couldn't have salvaged it if he'd wanted to. He had, with shocking ease, forgotten what this was all about. He wouldn't again.

Tense, he yanked open the door. The rain, now light, swirled around him, but he hardly noticed.

"Dillon?" Sami stood quickly, looking confused. "What's the matter?"

"I'm leaving," he said curtly, his gut tightening. He would *not* be affected by her look of hurt surprise, by the way her tall, lithe body swayed toward his.

"But it's still raining."

"Yeah, and it's cold too. But I prefer it to this." He paused when she looked as if he'd slapped her in the face, but he hardened his heart and shut the door behind him.

Staring at the door in bewilderment, Sami ran their last conversation through her mind, then stopped, frozen in dread. At the sight of the photos, her worst fears were confirmed. Dillon had seen the letters and the photographs.

And, judging by his violent reaction, he knew exactly what those photos were.

Sami went into work very early the next morning after having spent a sleepless night. Lucy and Felicia hadn't come in yet, and she made her way through the dim lobby, flipping on lights as she went. Of the two planes parked out front, one was Clark's.

Good. He'd be leaving then.

She walked through the hangar with the intention of confronting Dillon. She couldn't go on until she did. Some of the wind came out of her sail when she realized he wasn't yet in. Remembering the previous day when she'd been caged in with Clark, she opened the shades to both sides of the office. Now she could see into the hangar as well as down the rainy airstrip.

She plopped down on Dillon's desk and dropped her head in her hands. How could she be foolish enough to fall for a man like Dillon Kinley? He wore such a tough exterior, but she had glimpsed another side of him that appealed to her. He readily lent his time, his strength, his expertise to anyone who needed him, even her maintenance department. She'd seen him be kind and patient with Lucy, who helped him with secretarial services, even when that help was sporadic due to her heavy workload. To anyone who came through Reed Aviation, he was always upbeat and charming.

But nothing could change the fact that those appealing personality traits didn't always apply to her. She wished she understood why. She wanted answers.

Later, she couldn't remember how many minutes she'd sat there until a strange feeling, almost a premonition, overcame her. She raised her head and a scream ripped from her throat.

Coming at her, from outside on the airstrip, raced a large twin-jet airplane. Not even twenty feet away, it came barreling toward the building, directly at the window she stared out of. Eerily, through the fog, it charged, the cockpit empty.

Instinct raised her from her seat, but she could only back up against the wall before the plane careened in. She crouched down and covered her head with her arms a split second before the plane crumpled the metal exterior of the wall like a tin can and shot glass from the window across the room.

The sound deafened her.

EIGHT

Sami opened her eyes tentatively, surprised to find herself in one piece. The plane had rammed into the building so quickly that her heart rate just now reacted, drumming harshly against her ribs. She stood up, listening to the tinkle of glass as it fell off her body onto the floor.

The entire nose of the aircraft stuck through the wall of the office, extending to within inches of Dillon's desk where she'd been sitting.

She still stood there, panting with shock and disbelief, when the door of the office crashed open and Dillon rushed through. He skidded to a stop when he saw her, his eyes quickly scanning her, taking in her obviously disheveled state.

"Oh, God. You were in here." He moved quickly toward her, and carefully, with gentle fingers, he brushed loose glass off her face and body. "Are you hurt?"

She shook her head, not trusting her voice.

He touched her hair, wincing at the glass she knew

would be deeply embedded in the tangles. He swore, reached behind her, and dusted the glass off the nearest chair. Then pushed her into it.

Ricardo, Felicia, and two line crewmen crowded into the office, all talking at once. She felt Dillon possessively grip the back of her chair.

Lucy gasped from the doorway. "Are you all right? What happened?"

Sami managed to find her voice. "I was just sitting here waiting for Dillon. The next thing I know, this plane is on the loose and headed straight for me. I had time to jump away from the desk, but that's it."

Ricardo moved forward, touching her arm in sympathy. She tried to smile and failed. He shook his head at the mess, at the nose of the plane sticking through the wall. "I've never seen anything like it."

"It rolled from where it was parked?" Felicia asked.

Sami nodded. She could see the decline from the airstrip to where the building lay. With the ground so slick from the rain, it was easy to see how the plane had come to move so fast, especially given its weight.

All eyes turned to the desk where the plane had finally lost its momentum. Even with the window gone, shattered around the room, and the opening completely blocked by the plane, they could hear faint voices from the other side of the wall.

"I'm going to find me that damn pilot and see who didn't properly chock their plane."

"Wait a minute, Ricardo." Sami struggled to think clearly. "If the plane came in before the line crew came on, the pilot may have had to park the plane alone. And with the rain coming down as it is, maybe it was done incorrectly. Accidents can happen, especially here."

Dillon made a noise that she ignored.

"Still doesn't excuse it." Ricardo left after instructing Felicia to call security and the fire department, which they were required to do under FAA regulations.

"You could have been killed." Lucy hugged her.

"I'm not even hurt."

Dillon ran his gaze over her, heating her with that look. Clark came in, and Dillon stiffened beside her but remained silent.

"The entire side of the building has caved in. Whose plane is that?" He subjected Dillon to a scathing gaze that was returned. "The whole structure is ruined. That million-dollar plane is going to need a new front end." He shook his head. "What else is there to say?"

Dillon, still hovering too close for comfort, frowned fiercely. "How about, 'Sami, are you okay?'"

"What were you doing in here?" Clark came toward her, and she had to force herself not to cringe away.

"Don't touch her. Don't *ever* touch her."

The warning came from Dillon, but it was Lucy who moved in front of Clark, blocking the way. "Customers aren't really allowed back here, Mr. Viewmont," she said sweetly into the thick tension. "There's coffee in the lobby."

Sami reached for Lucy's hand and squeezed it gratefully. She met Dillon's incredibly intense gaze. It was also filled with unexpected compassion and tenderness. He cared. So did Lucy, and they'd banded together for her. The lump in her throat had nothing to do with her fright. But she had to stand up for herself.

"Business as usual, Clark," she said, her eyes still on Dillon. "Take it to the lobby."

Sirens sounded, and she reluctantly broke the eye contact. Outside she saw firsthand the awesome sight of the jet stuck into the side of the building as if it were a broken toy. The nose of the plane had been submerged into the building, completely buried, and the entire length of the wall had caved in.

Sometime in the past few minutes, the rain had stopped. In the early morning fog, water dripped off the plane into puddles on the wet concrete. In the cold air, she wrapped her arms about herself and stared at one of the strangest sights she'd ever seen.

Two hours later, Sami collapsed into a spare chair in Dillon's office. The plane had turned out to belong to a regular customer, and the pilot swore he'd properly tied the plane down.

The insurance adjuster assured her Reed wasn't responsible for the damages to the building or the aircraft because they'd been officially closed. The FAA investigator decided since no one had been injured, and the plane hadn't been airborne, it wasn't their concern. However, his parting statement had given her the shudders.

He'd said, "I'm not going to open an investigation, but if you want to know what I think, something isn't right here. The pilot swears he chocked the plane, and given his experience, I tend to believe him. The slant of the hill is great, but that isn't a cause for that plane to have moved so fast. You should investigate this thoroughly in-house and check your safety procedures. It could have been much, much worse."

It could have been much worse. No one knew that better than her. She knew the vision of that plane hurtling toward her would haunt her for a long, long time. She shivered again.

"Here," a deep, gruff voice said, thrusting a cup of hot coffee into her hands. Dillon hunkered down in front of her, resting his hands on the arms of the chair, watching her carefully. His forearms were bare and filled with sinewy strength. She remembered what it felt like to have them wrapped around her, and some small, weak feminine part of her wanted to feel that sense of warm safeness again.

"Hanging in there?" His voice seemed carefully neutral, but when she lifted her gaze, she read the concern so evident in his light eyes. Yes, he was still deeply upset with her since the previous night, and mad at God knew what, but he cared.

"I'm okay." Their faces were level. She could have easily reached out and rubbed her hand against his rough cheek, she wanted to bad enough. But she had pride too.

"The investigator is right." His gaze roamed her face, as if checking for unseen injuries.

"About what? How lucky we are that no one got hurt? How expensive the damage is? How pathetic it is that there wasn't a line crew available to help that pilot land?" She set the cup down and rose from the chair, needing to separate herself from him. She was tired of yearning for something she couldn't put a name to.

He straightened. "All those things, yes. But mostly about how strange the circumstances are."

Their gazes met from across the room and time stopped. The airport, their differences, and all the un-explainable events that stood between them disappeared, leaving them alone with unspoken emotions so thick, they became a tangible thing.

The loud creaking startled them both as the plane budged slightly, and the moment was over. Sami knew that the insurance agent, Ricardo, and some others were on the other side of the wall, trying to get the plane out. She leaned back against Dillon's desk.

"Why were you waiting for me this morning?" He came toward her with that lean, athletic grace she so admired, placing a hand on either side of her hips. In another time and place, his aggressiveness might have scared her. It had the opposite effect now.

"Tell me, Sami. The truth for once."

She sighed loudly and pushed away from him. She much preferred the other, softer, more kind Dillon. The one who'd brushed the glass from her hair, offered quiet assurances in a soothing, calm voice, while his eyes alone conveyed his rage and concern for her.

The plane budged backward another inch. She could hear the faint efforts and struggles of the men on the outside. "I've never lied to you," she said carefully. "I'm not going to bother asking you if you can say the same."

He moved to the door. "Never mind. I'm very late for a flight. In fact, I'll be lucky if this doesn't affect my business."

The plane lurched backward a foot or so, and there came a loud cheer of triumph from the other side. Then Ricardo's angry voice called out, admonishing someone to be careful, an instant before a piece of the nose of the plane fell heavily to the office floor.

Sami flinched and Dillon's toughness drained instantly. With a long arm, he reached out and pulled her close. She went willingly, sighing against his hard chest when his arms encircled her tight. She stood there, locked in his comforting embrace long after her fright had vanished, unwilling to let go of the moment. His steady, solid heartbeat warmed her, and she shifted closer, encouraged by the immediate effect that had on his heart rate.

"Better?" he asked, his voice betraying nothing of the now frantic heartbeat beneath her cheek.

"Yes," she whispered, but didn't budge.

His arms tightened imperceptibly around her, giving away more than he knew. Then the rest of the jet gave and suddenly there was a huge gaping hole to the outside revealing Ricardo and three other men gazing in. She jerked back from Dillon, but he was much slower at retrieving his arms from around her. The other men grinned at their success. Ricardo frowned.

"Things are moving along, I see. Howard will be so pleased." Clark lounged in the doorway. "Sami, I'd like to talk to you."

It was the last thing she wanted to do, but she wanted Clark out, now.

"No," came Dillon's surprising intervention. "Ricardo can see to your needs."

"You have no idea what my needs are," Clark responded.

"Whatever they are, they can wait."

They were going to go at each other's throats if she didn't stop them. "I'll give you two minutes, Clark."

Sami went quickly out into the hall, hoping to avoid a major confrontation, but all Dillon did was give her a look she had no problem deciphering.

The truce had been shattered like the glass that still lay at her feet.

She waited until she and Clark were in the lobby before she spoke. "Obviously, I'm busy today. I'd appreciate it very much if you'd stop entering areas that are off-limits to customers. That includes Kinley Charters' office. Stop bullying my employees and myself. And I'd like you to stop commanding so much of my time."

"You lied to me," he said smoothly. "You specifically told me that your crew was now working a twenty-four-hour shift."

"So?"

"If that were true, this little accident wouldn't have happened." He lowered his voice to a soft whisper that gave her the chills. "Would it?"

It didn't help that he was right. "It has nothing to do with you."

"Doesn't it? What if something happens to my new plane on your property?"

"If you're worried, don't bring your plane here."

"You need me. The sooner you realize that, the better."

Anger surged through her, feeding her strength, and with it came a renewed sense of energy. He couldn't hurt her here. "Are you threatening me, Clark?"

"You will be sorry, Sami. I promise you that."

She repressed her shudder. She wasn't about to let anything ruin her chance to do something she loved, and to get to know the father she'd never spent time with. "I want you to stop reporting every little thing I do to my father. It's unacceptable." She set her hands on her desk. "Those are the rules. Play by them, and I'll continue to let you land."

Thirty minutes later she got a call from the hospital. Her father had just suffered another minor heart attack.

It couldn't be only ten o'clock at night, Sami thought. She drove away from the hospital after a lengthy and unsatisfactory visit with her father.

Clark had, of course, told him everything about the plane incident. And bless his weak heart, her father would be fine. But her growing sense that her father was involved with Clark in something he shouldn't be had grown. The second he was out of intensive care, she'd demand to know what.

The rain still fell, but she had to make sure the hole in Dillon's office had been properly boarded up so that the building was secure. She walked through the dark, deserted hangar, hearing someone hammering. Braving the wind and the rain, she walked down the airstrip to where the plane had hit the building.

Dillon slammed in a nail, tossed down the hammer, and stood back to survey his work. And work he had done. She could see at least ten sheets of plywood, maybe more, all stretched and nailed over the huge hole. He'd also pulled out the remaining glass from the window and covered that too. She knew better than to be surprised at anything this enigmatic man did, but she still felt astounded.

Although the air was chilly and wet, he wore nothing but a pair of Levi's jeans and a T-shirt. He stretched, making the sheer, wet shirt pull over his muscles in interesting ways. Her stomach fluttered. She wondered if those wonderful arms were as warm as they had been that morning when he'd held her.

"Satisfactory?" he asked without turning his head.

Sami gaped at his back. He'd known she was standing there, admiring his work. And his body. She felt the heat flood her face. "Very," she assured him, and his head whipped around to look at her. "You did a lot of hard work," she clarified with a slightly unsteady voice. "Thank you."

He nodded, his gaze holding hers. The wind hit and battered them, whirling noisily in between the buildings, creating a sort of cocoon that isolated them from the outside world. It struck Sami then that she hardly knew this man. He had layers to him that kept peeling off, exposing a new Dillon for her to discover. She'd seen him loose and carefree, charming and flirtatious, and yet she knew that boiling beneath the surface he sported a formidable temper that erupted at the slightest injustice.

"Who are you really, Dillon Kinley?" she asked softly.

He smiled a little. "Just a pilot trying to make a decent living."

She pulled her coat tighter about her when the wind threatened to rip it open. Her eyes were huge on his. "Why do I doubt that?"

He deserved her doubts but wasn't ready to tell all. "I think the question is, who are *you*?" He stepped closer to her, alarmed at how tired and dispirited she seemed. He wanted nothing more than to pick up where they'd left off that morning, with her encased so perfectly in his arms. But Clark had interrupted them, and she'd allowed it.

Sami Reed was full of contradictions. She fascinated him. He appreciated the way she managed her employees, treating them all equally and with the respect they deserved. He admired the way she could keep her cool in the toughest of circumstances. She stood firm in her beliefs, she was loyal to a fault, and she was the bravest woman he'd ever met. He wanted her more than he'd ever wanted another woman in his life.

And she held the secrets to his brother's death.

"I'm exactly what you see, Dillon. No more, no less."

"Now, why do I doubt that?" he said, mockingly repeating her words. They stared at each other in a mute impasse, the wind and rain pummeling them. She shivered and he sighed.

"Come on." He led her back to the dark lobby, and they each reached for the door at the same time. Their hands brushed together and they each pulled back quickly, staring stupidly at each other. He watched her breath quicken and imagined her pulse did too. Desire bolted through him, and it took every ounce of control he had not to reach for her.

"Thanks again for the help," she said, slipping her hands into her pockets. She glanced—longingly, he noticed with irritation—toward the front door.

She couldn't wait to leave him. Perversely, he detained her, knowing he wouldn't be satisfied until she felt every bit as frustrated and grumpy as he did.

"Someone had to," he remarked casually. "You left in a huff."

"My father was ill," she snapped, as piqued over the insult as he'd known she'd be. "Aren't you going to ask me about his health?"

The man would live, he'd already checked. "Nope."

She gasped, looking at him as if she didn't recognize him. He felt marginally better. He might as well go all the way and thoroughly tick her off. "So," he drawled, putting his hands on her hips and pulling her against his tight and aching body, "What were you so hot to tell me this morning when we were untimely interrupted?"

She took a step backward and glared at him with hostility. "I don't remember."

"Liar."

Her eyes narrowed. "Stop calling me that."

"Then stop lying."

"Stay out of my affairs!" With her hands on her hips, her hair wild and wet, and her eyes snapping from her anger, she looked marvelously in charge of her emotions.

"I can't do that."

"You said you would," she pressed, almost desperately.

"I did not."

She threw up her hands then. "Oh, please."

He regretted the bitter look she gave him, but he'd asked for it. "I changed my mind." He walked out the door then and didn't stop his flow of motion until he stood in his cabin, peeling off wet clothes. Then he turned the shower on steaming hot and bent under the flow of water, letting it bead off his back. He badly missed his loud, loving, boisterous family. He'd had the very best family ever—a very long time ago.

He was alone now. Completely, totally alone.

Exhaustion had set in by the time he stretched out on his bed. But sleep wouldn't come. He berated himself for taking out his anger and frustration on Sami. She hadn't deserved his harsh words. He should come clean with her. She'd tell him whatever she knew. Wouldn't she?

The last, lingering doubt held him back.

There will be another accident.

Sami stared at the plain white piece of paper she'd got in the mail. Her first thought was that it had come too late, given what had happened the day before. But her second thought was more dismal. What if it meant another accident, where someone got hurt—or worse? But her third thought brought her upright in her chair.

The letters hadn't started coming until Dillon Kinley had come to Reed Aviation. She slapped her hands down on her desk and stood. She had to talk to Dillon. Not banter. Not argue. Not play that silly dance around each other that they'd gotten so good at, but really talk. She wanted to know how he'd recognized Kevin's things, how he'd known what those pictures of Kevin's accident were. She wanted to know that he had nothing to do with the letters. She wanted to know why he seemed so interested in her problems.

She needed to know if he felt half the helpless attraction for her that she felt for him.

"Sami?" Lucy stood in the doorway with a frazzled and harassed look. "Do you have a minute?"

She didn't, but for Lucy, she'd find one. "Of course."

Lucy shut the door. "I'm worried. About you."

"Oh," she said with a little relieved laugh. This she could handle. "I'm fine. Not a scratch on me from yesterday."

"But will you stay fine?" Lucy's even gaze met hers. "I saw the letter, Sami," she said quickly, wringing her hands. "I was screening the mail for you and I read it by accident. I wasn't trying to pry."

Sami sighed. "It's all right." She told her about the others.

Lucy blanched. "I think you should know that I believe Kevin's death wasn't an accident."

Sami stared at her in surprise. "Why didn't you ever say anything?"

"I don't know. Maybe I should have. But I've always believed something other than pilot error caused that crash. He was . . . too good," she said simply.

Sami's smile was sad. "You cared for him very much."

"Yes," she whispered. "So much. And I never got to tell him." Her eyes filled with tears. "I wish we could understand what's happening."

"Me too," she murmured. "Me too."

Sami found Dillon in the last place she expected—working on her mother's plane.

His lower body hung out of the engine compartment—and what a lower body it was. Powerful, long, lean. Her clicking heels alerted him to her presence, and he straightened from the plane, watching without a word as she approached, slowly wiping his hands on a cloth from his hip pocket. How did a man look so damn good wearing a pair of dirty green mechanic's overalls?

"What are you doing?" she asked, slightly breathless.

He tossed his rag aside and cocked his head toward the plane. "You're right. She'll fly."

She'd been armed with questions, yet she found herself strangely tongue-tied. "Good."

"Ready?"

His eyes shined with an emotion she couldn't place. "For what?"

"A test flight."

"Now?"

"Why not?" He gave her a beguiling open smile that completely disarmed her.

It wasn't the first time she'd wanted to question his sanity. *Or hers.* "Where would we go?"

"Let's wing it," he suggested with the careless shrug of a man who couldn't possibly be tied down to something as mundane as a flight plan. "Okay?"

She thought about the stacks upon stacks of work back on her desk, but this was a Dillon she'd never been able to resist. Then he unzipped his mechanic's overalls and looked at her as he peeled them slowly off. Her mouth went dry, even though he wore jeans and a T-shirt beneath. "Okay, Sami?" he asked again, using that same husky, intimate tone he'd used when he'd kissed her. Her knees went weak.

It should be illegal to have a body like that, she decided. "Um . . . okay."

"I'd have to change first," he said, giving her a hot look, now tinged with humor. He knew damn well what he'd done to her.

"I'll just . . . wait here." Far too proud to let him see how he affected her, she smiled coolly, though her legs wobbled. She managed to back to a chair and plop down without falling.

He laughed. He laughed and walked to the locker room.

Five minutes later, in the cockpit, Dillon flipped on a pair of sunglasses and talked quietly into his headset to the control tower. His strong, sure hands hit the various switches required for takeoff, and Sami found herself enthralled by the process she'd witnessed thousands of times before.

Not often did she act so spontaneously as to take off without a word or warning in the middle of a workday, but the rush of adrenaline she'd gotten from it gave her a zesty feeling for life she hadn't experienced in too long. She felt giddy with it and laughed softly with sheer pleasure as she watched Bear Pass fade away in the distance.

"What's so funny?"

"This is fun."

He laughed. "You sound surprised."

"My mother would have loved this. A spontaneous flight in her favorite plane." She sighed. "I miss her."

His eyes were solemn. "You're not close to your father?"

She laughed a little. "Not exactly. I grew up on the East Coast. I only really got to know him in these past six months or so." Realizing she knew next to nothing about him, she asked, "How about you? Nice family?"

"The best."

It might have been the coziness of the cockpit. The isolation certainly helped. But being surrounded by nothing but wide-open sky lent an air of camaraderie between them that they'd never experienced before.

"Tell me about them."

"My parents are dead."

Given the ironic twist to his mouth and harshly set features, she could imagine how much that admission cost him. "Is there no one else? Brothers or sisters?"

He sighed. "Nope."

"I'm sorry." She shouldn't have pried, she thought. Now she'd never get back that easy mood between them.

"It was a long time ago."

"But it still hurts," she guessed. She knew that one firsthand.

He stared at her for several heartbeats. His eyes seemed incredibly green. "Yes," he said softly. "It still hurts." His next words tore at her heart. "They died in a plane crash."

"Oh, Dillon."

"My dad was a pilot. They flew all the time. He took Mom to Mammoth Mountain, but on their way home they hit a storm. They went down, and no one could find the wreck for days." He shrugged. "They froze to death."

"Were you close?"

"Very."

And yet another layer peeled away. They'd flown

southwest, and now she could see the Pacific Ocean on the horizon. She couldn't see the gas gauge, but she knew they wouldn't be able to go much farther and get back. "Are we almost there?"

"Yep." He'd say nothing more.

NINE

Sami took a deep breath. "There's some things I really need to talk to you about."

"Good," Dillon said. "Me too."

"Okay," she said uneasily. "What is it?"

"You'll have to wait until we get—" He maneuvered the plane in a sharp right-hand turn that had her gripping the dash and peering out the cockpit window nervously. "There," he said.

"There" was the sharp jutting expanse of mountain range that was the island of Catalina. The island was small, the airport positively tiny. For even a skilled pilot, Santa Catalina Island's narrow landing strip could be a challenge, but not to Dillon. When he'd executed the tight landing and finally stopped the plane, he turned to Sami.

She opened her eyes slowly, releasing white knuckles from the dash and taking a deep breath. He chuckled at the look on her face. "You okay?"

"Of course." She raised her chin in that endearing, stubborn way of hers. "What are we doing?"

"Haven't you been here before?"

She looked out of the cockpit at the deep forest and steep mountain range around her. "No."

He struggled to smile easily at the ever-defensive woman next to him. Of course she hadn't, she never took time to enjoy herself. "Well, you're here now."

"Great." She grumbled as he helped her down from the cockpit. But she fell quiet as they strolled through the quaint town of Avalon. Cruise lines made this quaint town a regular stop on their route, so that even now, as winter came, the streets were filled with people shopping.

He loved this place. Loved the eclectic group of people, loved the hustle and bustle, loved the smell of the sea as he walked. He pulled Sami into a little café on one corner, where they got a table overlooking the marina. He ordered them brunch, and they sat watching the vast variety of fishing vessels, sailboats, and yachts pull into the docks.

Sami took a sip of iced tea and sighed with pleasure. "I should be stressed about being away from work, but I'm not."

It made him ridiculously pleased that he could give her a taste of the luxury that she so rarely allowed herself.

He was digging himself in deeper and deeper by falling for this woman whom he'd lied to repeatedly. A woman he could only hope was as innocent of the death of his brother as she seemed. He had no idea what would happen when this was all over, but for now, he wanted to be near her. He was beginning to suspect he'd always feel that way. He watched her take a long sip of her tea. Her tongue played with the straw, and the physical ache she invariably caused in him throbbed.

She shifted uneasily in her chair and played with the tablecloth. "What are you nervous about?" he asked.

She lowered her eyes. "You must have brought me here for a reason."

He didn't answer immediately, because she pulled at her sweaterdress, making it tight across her breasts, giving him a tantalizing glimpse of her perfect, softly curved shape.

"You wanted to take up your mother's plane, and so did I."

She shot him a look of exasperation. "But—"

"No buts. Why do you look for a way to turn everything into work? Just enjoy the day. Or the minute for that matter."

She looked startled that he knew her so well. It made him smile. "There's no ulterior motive, Sami." He reached for her hand across the table. "Just enjoy."

"I can't. Not when there's so much between us."

He sighed. He guessed his fantasy of kissing her until she relaxed against him, all wariness gone from those lovely hazel eyes, wasn't going to happen today.

"When we got stuck in the elevator, you acted as if maybe you recognized the things in the duffel bag. And then, the other night at my house, you left in a hurry."

He leaned back in his chair, his long legs stretched out in front of him with one arm thrown haphazardly across the table. Yet she knew from the sudden intenseness of his eyes and the way his other hand fisted about his glass that he didn't feel nearly as relaxed as he would have her believe.

"Go on," he said softly.

"The letters, Dillon. And the pictures. You've seen them before."

His chin dropped to his chest. Neither of them moved. Finally, he raised his gaze back to hers. "I recognized them. Why are you hiding them instead of having them investigated?"

"You think they're real? I figured them as a scare tactic."

"You're taking an awfully big chance on the assumption."

She laughed shakily. "There was an investigation. It was an accident. An *accident*, Dillon. There was no foul play." She thought uneasily of the last letter. "It's someone's idea of a sick joke."

"Whose?" he demanded.

"Probably Clark." She eyed him cautiously. "Or . . ."

"Or?"

His eyes dared her. "You. It could be you."

"That'd be convenient for you, Sami." He shook his head. "Sorry to disappoint you."

"Am I supposed to take your word for that?"

"No, you're not." He leaned forward, making breathing next to impossible. "That's the point. You shouldn't take anyone's word. You should get to the bottom of it. To why Kevin died."

"Which brings us back to the original question. Why do you care?"

"Someone should," he retorted, bringing his glass to his lips.

He had nerve. Just the accusation made her eyes sting. "If you're suggesting that I don't care—guess again. I care more than you could possibly know."

He looked at her for a long moment. "Then why haven't you done anything about the fact that something is definitely out of sync at Reed?" he asked quietly.

She wanted to, he had no idea how much she wanted to. And if she were being honest, she'd have to admit that her fear for her father's involvement grew daily. She leaned back and sighed. "This is ridiculous. You aren't going to tell me anything."

"And neither are you."

They watched each other in mute distrust until the waitress removed their plates. Dillon tossed some money down on the table and pulled her to her feet. "Come on. We've got some sight-seeing left to do."

"I don't want to." The magic had fled.

He took her shoulders in his hands, stooping down when she stubbornly refused to make eye contact. "Hey," he said softly, shaking her lightly until she looked at him. "What's the worst that could happen now? You could have fun?"

"I'm not finished talking to you—"

"No, we're not finished. Not by a long shot. Come?"

They rented a golf cart for transportation since cars weren't allowed on the island. Dillon drove them up a breathtaking, bumpy, narrow road with a rocky mountain on the left and a sheer drop-off to the Pacific Ocean on the right.

"This road isn't wide enough if another cart comes down the other way," she said in alarm, gripping the dash for dear life.

If he was trying to miss the huge potholes, he wasn't succeeding. "Don't worry. It's usually a one-way."

"Usually?" she squeaked. "Great. Just great."

He maneuvered them up and over a sharp set of jackknife turns that no car could have possibly handled. As they rose, the deep blue sky seemed to get closer and the white puffs of clouds seemed bigger and lower. The lush green mountains surrounded them. The brilliant jade of the ocean glimmered below. At the very top, Dillon stopped.

"What do you think?"

They were on top of the world. She looked down on the bay where the town of Avalon sat nestled in the cove. "It's lovely," she admitted.

He hopped out of the cart and led her to a small path, nearly hidden by brush. "The view is even better this way." At the top of the trail sat a bench, shaded by two large trees.

"I've never seen anything so beautiful in all my life."

"I know," he said. "This is one of my favorite places."

She looked at the ocean, wondering how many women he'd flown here. "Come often?"

"Not as often as I'd like." He turned her face to his. "And always alone. It's much better this way. With you."

He shouldn't look at her that way, as if she were the only woman on earth. Her stomach did that strange flutter. She looked away first. The top of the world was a noisy place: birds chattered, bushes rustled with the breeze, insects buzzed.

"Sami?" He ran a finger along the furrow between her eyebrows. It relaxed the crease that was always there when she thought too much. "Don't be afraid of me."

She looked at him—a mistake. How could she explain that the feelings he evoked in her terrified her? That she'd never, ever felt this strange, delicious, and fuzzy feeling before? That he knocked her for such a loop, she'd never find her way out? Despite the wonderfully cool breeze that gently ruffled her hair, she felt warm. Too warm. "I—I'm not."

He brought his mouth to hers lightly. "I wanted to talk to you here." He kissed her again. "But every time I get this close, I feel like doing something else."

"Dillon—"

The rest of her words were lost as his lips grazed hers once, then again, before tracing a trail to her ear. He tugged on the sensitive lobe with his teeth, and a little sound escaped her. She struggled with control, but lost that fight when he pulled her close against him. She went willingly, clutching his shoulders, yearning and aching, and wishing she didn't. But how could she resist, when he tasted exactly the way he smelled—heavenly and pure male.

The next kiss wasn't short or gentle, but hot, deep, and wet. He pulled her on his lap before she could protest, fitting her snugly to his thighs. His lips nuzzled at her throat, his hands held her hips close to his. Cursing softly, he shifted beneath her. Her gaze flew to his, shocked.

"Yeah," he murmured, as she became intensely aware of his erection, "that's what you do to me."

She went to move, but he held her still, bringing his lips back to hers. Her insides hummed like the bees around her. She really couldn't think, but when his hands encircled her waist, then rested high on her ribs, reality returned. Pushing shakily against his chest, she straightened. "You're very distracting, Dillon."

"What?" His tongue laid a fresh assault against her senses, tracing a path over her neck. His thumbs brushed the underside of her breasts, and she sucked in her breath.

His caressing fingers smoothed back her scoop collar so he could kiss the base of her neck where her pulse beat frantically. "Please," she said with a gasp.

"Please what, Sami?" His voice was deep, sexy, and he continued his trail of hot kisses as he slowly peeled back her sweaterdress. "Just tell me what you want, it's yours." His mouth was at the top of her breast now, and her bones had dissolved.

"I want—Oh, God." Through the lace, his tongue found her.

"You want . . . ?" His fingers followed suit, teasing her hard nipples. His gaze, hot and hungry, followed his movements.

She had to do this before she lost it completely. "I want you to tell me how you know so much about Kevin."

He blinked his desire-clouded eyes into focus. "What?"

Self-consciously, she moved off his lap to the bench, smoothing the top of her dress back into place. She took a deep breath against the raging desire enclosing her and Dillon in an intimacy she couldn't control. She had to be blunt. "I don't think the runaway plane was an accident."

That got his attention. "That makes two of us." He

leaned back on the bench in a relaxed pose, recovering from their kisses annoyingly quick.

She stood. "Are you sending the letters, Dillon?"

His eyes glinted dangerously as he also stood. "*What?*"

"You're the type of man who's capable of just about anything."

He laughed in amazement. "Letters aren't my style, Sami."

"Can't you just deny it? Tell me you didn't do it? Tell me, Dillon. Tell me that my hunch that you know more than you're letting on is wrong!"

He let out another short laugh. "Why? Would you believe it?"

"I might," she said seriously. "You're hiding something. I can feel it." The molding of his features gave nothing of his thoughts away. "What are you really doing in Bear Pass, Dillon?"

"You're not going to like it."

"Try me."

He stared out to sea for a long moment. Finally, he turned back to her, his eyes brimming with regret and pain. "You're not ready to hear it."

Without a word, she walked around him and headed down the path. At the cart, he tried once more. "Sami—"

"Forget it, Dillon. The truth is, you don't owe me any explanations, any more than I owe you. Let's just drop it and get back to work."

"But—"

"You do charters, don't you?"

"Of course," he said, confused by the question.

"Well then charter me the hell out of here."

Those were the last words they exchanged the entire way back.

Dillon stalked his office that night, briefly touching the still boarded up area that had once been his window to the airstrip. Things had gotten much more complicated than he'd ever planned on. Now he had Sami to worry about on top of this heavily woven mess he'd created.

He'd never forget that stunned surprise on her face when the shelving unit had barely missed smashing her into the concrete floor. Nor her sheer terror after the near miss with the runaway plane. Both were seemingly bizarre accidents. But he knew better.

Had his arrival and questions about Kevin stirred someone up? The killer perhaps? Had he inadvertently put Sami in danger? He sighed as he left his office. The next day was Thanksgiving. It used to be his favorite time of year. His family would gather. They'd laugh, they'd fight. They'd love.

This year would be quite different.

This year, for the first time in his life, the forceful wanderlust within him had fled. No longer did he want to travel the world alone, searching for adventure. No longer did he want to leave Bear Pass. He liked his charter, liked running his own business, and especially liked being his own boss for a change. But there was more.

He wanted a family.

The thought startled him, but the fact remained. He wanted the intimacy that came from loving and being loved. He wanted children.

He wanted Sami Reed. Forever.

He couldn't have her. She'd never forgive him for his duplicity. Someone else wanted her, too, only they wanted her *out* of the picture. Permanently.

He still had to figure out who, before it was too late.

Sami awoke before dawn on Thanksgiving morning, haunted by the memories of Thanksgiving's past. Her mother had loved the holiday, surprising as that was, since she'd never cooked a day in her life. Even so, she'd always made it special.

Sami missed her horribly.

She showered and dressed in her favorite weekend wear: jeans and a pullover sweater. Since she'd accepted none of the invitations she'd gotten from friends, the day loomed long in front of her.

Without warning, she thought of Dillon. She hadn't been fair, any more than he had. She owed him an apology. Not stopping to think, she grabbed her keys and headed out. She drove, resolutely keeping her mind blank, refusing to allow herself to think about what she was doing.

It had rained during the night. The roads had iced over. They were dangerous enough to drive under the best of circumstances; her state of mind made the act reckless. The first inkling of doubt didn't come until she pulled into his driveway. Maybe he had plans. Maybe he had company. Maybe, since it was still very early, he slept. An unbidden image of him doing just that, all rumpled and lying twisted in his bedsheets, had her stomach doing that flutter again.

"You're ridiculous," she muttered to herself, walking up the driveway.

Dillon answered the door looking more wonderfully tousled than she could have imagined, and enormously sexy in Levi's jeans and nothing else.

She'd surprised him. His eyes flickered over her, ending at the pale blush that she could feel on her face. He leaned against the doorjamb and crossed his arms over his bare chest. His voice sounded deep and husky with sleep. "Sami. What are you doing here?"

TEN

Sami returned Dillon's steady gaze with difficulty. She didn't have much experience with nearly nude men, especially one so . . . *gorgeously* nearly nude. And to make everything worse, she couldn't remember exactly what had brought her out to his house. His look told her he didn't know if he was thrilled or irritated at the sight of her.

She knew exactly how he felt. "Can I come in?"

He raised his eyebrows, but made no further comment as he moved aside. Her shoulder brushed against his bare chest, her hand against a denim-clad thigh as she walked past him. A hot and dangerous current ran between them.

Concentrating on the inside of his cabin helped. It was small, but so utterly warm and comfortable that she immediately felt at home, despite her inner turmoil. The furnishings were simple and rustic, perfect in their cabin setting. Snug and cozy. A fire crackled from the large brick fireplace, giving off more warmth and light.

He shut the front door and leaned back against it, careful to maintain a safe distance.

"You're probably wondering why I'm here," she said awkwardly into the silence.

Laughter filled his eyes. "Breakfast?" he asked in a rough-timbered voice with a note of hope in it.

That, matched with the suggestive expression on his face, caused her heart to start a slow, heavy beat. She couldn't remember the flimsy excuse that had brought her there, but he looked far too sexy for his own good. She didn't trust him or herself at the moment, so with newfound purpose, she reached past him for the door handle, intending to get as far away from the man as she could.

She tried to get out but he was broad, solid, and completely immovable. She raised her gaze to his and was horrified to see he no longer looked grim and uncertain—he grinned from ear to ear.

"Move!" she ordered, tugging uselessly at the door. Her fingers brushed against the warm skin of his sleek back, and she pulled her hand away abruptly.

"Not until you tell me why you're here."

She shook her head stubbornly. Smiling pleasantly, as though he found an uneager female at his door every day, he bent down and looked in her ear. "Supposedly there's a great sense of humor lurking in there someplace."

She slapped at his hands. "Knock it off."

He sighed. "Someday, Sami, you're going to tell a joke, and I'm going to fall over in shock."

She stepped back from his disturbing closeness, refusing to allow her gaze to feast on that magnificent chest.

"Tell me what's up," he urged. "I'll be good. . . ." He trailed off the promise with an intimately low voice and a suggestive lift of his brows.

Her heart skipped a beat. "Not likely," she returned with clenched teeth.

"Try me." His smile was still in place, but something much, much more potent than humor swam in his eyes.

She gave up. "To tell you the truth, I really have no idea why I'm here."

His smile faded, and his voice was quiet. "I do."

A helpless laugh escaped her. "You'd better tell me then."

Her heart beat hard and heavy in her chest. She wished he wore a shirt so she couldn't see his wide, tight chest and flat, hard stomach. She wished his jeans had been buttoned all the way, or that they didn't reveal every contour in his long legs and lean hips. She wished he wouldn't look at her with such naked longing, because it made her ache for what she couldn't—wouldn't—have.

"I'll just show you," he said, reaching for her. The concentrated look on his face hadn't been there before, and with it she saw something else, something equally unnerving—his own doubt and fear. Her heart leaped as he touched his mouth to hers.

She meant to stop him, she really did. She wasn't very good at this, had never considered herself especially sexual. But stopping became impossible. The kiss felt right, as necessary at that moment as air to her lungs. They were all alone, together, with no demands on them other than the ones they placed there themselves. The isolation only lent to the strong hunger, the desperate need.

He tasted warm, sweet, and oh, so right. Her arms crept up around his shoulders, over the bare, hot skin she'd been craving to touch. She held tight. He nibbled at the corners of her mouth until she opened it for him. Her insides hummed, her head swam, her bones seemed to melt away, and yet a sense of uncertainty lingered, an uncertainty that must have matched his own.

Slowly, they drew back, as purposefully and carefully as they'd met. Dillon's intent face held an expression that neared pain. Sami knew hers held confusion.

Dillon cursed softly into the silence. "I didn't want this," he whispered hoarsely, resting his hands on her shoulders. "I didn't want to want you so much . . . so damn much."

"But you do," she breathed, startled and . . . turned on by the thought that it was *her* making his skin quiver. She had only to press against his hardened body to know how aroused he was. That this vital, resilient man could become weak from wanting her excited her beyond belief. "You do want me and . . ."

"And?"

"And I want you." They came together again for another hot, searing, wild kiss that awakened a driving hunger she had to fulfill. She loved the taste of him, loved the feel of his strong hands sliding up and down her spine, loved the low sound of satisfaction that she wrung from him whenever she arched against him.

God, she could love this man—if she let herself.

He kept kissing her, and she clung to him, helplessly lost in the swirling sensation vibrating through her body. She needed more. She clasped his hips and rubbed her own against them, unprepared for his reaction. He groaned, then spun her around, sandwiching her between the cold door and his hard, warm body.

"I promised myself I wouldn't do this," he rasped against her neck, streaking his hands beneath her sweater. Her mind stopped, simply stopped. She couldn't think with those greedy hands on her. While he spread openmouthed kisses over her neck, his hands cupped her breasts, and if she thought she couldn't breathe before, she had never been so wrong. His tongue on her ear had shivers moving down her spine. The leg he thrust between hers, gliding denim along the most sensitive part of her, threw her senses into overdrive.

"Or this," he said thickly, pushing her sweater up and kissing the soft skin where it swelled out of her lacy bra. The pad of his thumb slid slowly back and forth over a covered nipple, startling a gasp from her. Her head lolled back against the door, allowing his mouth greater access, which he took full advantage of.

"And I refused even to think about doing this," he whispered hoarsely, unbuttoning her jeans and sliding a hand inside to cup her bottom.

She clutched him in curious desperation. The anticipation became tangible. She whispered his name in stunned awe.

"Be sure, Sami." He held her tight and closed his eyes. "You've got to be sure."

"Yes," she managed as he softly kissed one breast. He drew the tightened, aching point into his mouth, sucking hard. "Lord, yes."

His fingers slid beneath the lace edging of her panties, then found the heat of her, stroking once at the place that set off little shock waves. Her throat closed up, and she pressed her hips against his in an unspoken appeal. He inhaled sharply at the contact and touched her again, lightly, until she twisted against him, digging her nails into his back. "Dillon—"

"Not here," he said gruffly, and lifted her, cradling her to his wonderfully solid, warm chest. Up the stairs they went, stopping for deep, drugging kisses, then on to his loft bedroom, where he set her by his huge, un-made bed. He pushed back her hair, then fit his hand to the soft slant of her neck. His thumb stroked her jaw as he searched her face. "Last chance."

Sun streamed in from the skylight above, warming the room. She smelled spice, clean clothes, and the fire from below. She looked at him. His body was rigid, tensed for her rejection. He needed her. She could no more deny him than herself.

"I want you," she said, and his entire body relaxed. He smiled at her, a sweet, affectionate and open smile she'd never seen before. She closed her eyes to the bright sunlight while his other hand slid up her throat to frame her face. He kissed her, a long kiss that held a promise of things to come. The urgency came back tenfold as he pulled her down beside him on his softly rumpled bed.

He rolled her beneath him, towering above her, stopping her breath with his unwavering gaze. "I've wanted you from that first day I saw you standing in the lobby, dripping wet." His eyes seemed unusually green in the bright, warm sunlight. "I've wanted you ever since." Her insides ached inexplicably, and she reached for him, pulling him down to her, loving the feel of his arms as they surrounded her. He closed his eyes, but they flashed open again and pierced her with a hungry gaze. "But I've never wanted you more than I do right now." He claimed her mouth again, lingering there, mouth to mouth, body pressed to body, until she sank back into the wonderful haziness of arousal and need.

She had no choice but to feel, to touch in return. Her pulse raced, her heart pounded, her muscles trembled. He pulled her sweater over her head, and despite herself, she froze up. He kissed her softly, over and over again until she relaxed.

She slid her hands over his chest, and her name tumbled from his lips. Empowered, she trailed fingertips down, down, to the front of his jeans, then after a brief hesitation, she unfastened them. He watched her as she peeled his jeans away, her eyes riveted by what she exposed. He let out a moaning laugh and kneeled, meeting her in the center of the bed.

His hot tongue trailed over her body as streams of light poured over the top of them from above. She clasped his head to her and sighed as he separated her lace bra with unsteady hands. Their gazes met, held, as he slid her jeans down over her hips. She'd never felt more vulnerable or aroused in her life.

"Ah, Sami, you're lovely," he whispered. "So lovely." And she felt it. Her hands slid around his waist, his into her hair.

Longing and a flicker of something she didn't understand flashed into his eyes as he dragged her head back and crushed his lips to hers. He ran his teeth over her shoulder, and her head fell back. She couldn't catch her breath. He pressed her back to the soft comforter that smelled so good, so like him, and covered her body with his. He smiled, and her heart melted. But when he leaned down and gently, purposefully, took a nipple in his teeth, she gasped, arching beneath him.

The fire crackling below was the only noise except for Sami's low moan as Dillon smoothed fingers down over her ribs, her stomach. She held her breath. He moved them lower, playing with her, feathering her lightly, in a teasing motion she couldn't stand, but couldn't bear if he stopped. She whispered his name and writhed beneath him, clutching his shoulders in fisted hands. If he quit, she'd scream. She clamped her legs tight over his hand, imprisoning him, and he laughed at her softly. "Dillon," she whispered, frantic.

"Shhh. It's all right." His fingers never let up their delicious torment. "Let me show you. Let me drive you crazy." He kissed her slowly while his fingers did just that. She cried out, gripping the sheet at her sides in sweaty fists. "Is it working?" he asked thickly.

"I—Yes," she gasped, half-afraid he'd stop. "But—"

He kissed her words away, his magic fingers driving her senseless, taking her to a place she'd never been before, and then, even before her breath had slowed, he began again until she was quivering beneath him.

Damp flesh slid over damp flesh as he moved up her body, but she felt weightless, hardly aware of anything but the crazy sense of relief he'd created. She couldn't have moved to save her life. "I guess I liked it," she said in awe, staring into his smoldering, heavy-lidded gaze.

"We're not through, Sami," he said unevenly. "Not by a long shot." And he plunged into her, shooting her from contentment to a renewed ruthless need in that split second. No more gentle teasing, but a hunger past enduring. She lifted her hips to meet his, watching his face grimace in pleasure. She'd never felt like this, so . . . wildly, helplessly needy. They rolled over the bed, grappling and frenzied, until he captured her beneath him and held her face in his hands. Within her, he leaped and pulsed. "I've dreamed of this," he told her, his voice thick and tight. "I've dreamed of this for so long."

He lowered his mouth to hers and took her.

The fire below had turned to smoldering ashes, and the sun above had shifted when Sami stirred at his side.

He concentrated on her heart beating erratically against his while he gently touched her, exploring the slender body he was coming to know and, yes, love. She lifted her head and gazed at him with those gorgeous eyes, and he knew he hadn't had nearly enough. He pulled her on top of him, whispering her name. She smiled, more than ready. He dragged a moan from her as he stroked her breasts, her belly, and she bucked and arched when he slid his fingers between her thighs.

"Does this mean," she panted, "we're still not through?"

"No," he whispered, "there's more. I'll show you." He put his thumb to the apex of her thighs. She stroked her hands down over her own slick body, a look of astonished delight and arousal on her face, then groped his shoulders in a grip of steel when he slowly, deliberately, pressed against the little nub there. Her eyes fell closed, and she pressed forward against his hand, undulating her hips. Wave after wave of sensations rolled over him as he watched her take her own pleasure. "Look at me," he demanded, bringing her face down for a kiss. "This is more," he said, thrusting into her, meeting her stunned and dazed eyes. "This is more." And he began to move.

The sun slanted over their damp bodies. Sami lay collapsed over Dillon's chest, limp. He had no regrets.

Certainly not after what he'd discovered the night before, after he'd left the airport. It had changed everything. He had to tell her, share what he'd learned, but selfishly, he wanted to keep this time between them personal as long as he could.

He had to smile at how she looked, sprawled wantonly over the top of him, her skin glowing, her body replete. He could lay in this heap of entwined limbs, stroking her body forever, if she'd let him. He sank his fingers into her tangled hair, fingering the silky strands. At his touch, she tightened her arms around him, leaving her eyes closed. She couldn't know what that did to his heart, having her hold him that way.

"How do you do it?" he asked.

She opened her eyes, then reached out a hand to trace the outline of his lips. "Do what?"

He kissed her fingers. "Turn me upside down with just a touch."

The wary look he'd kissed away only moments before came back. "Is that good or bad?"

"I'm not certain." He grinned. "Do it again, and I'll try to figure it out."

She eased herself off him and sat up, pulling the sheet up to her chin. He might have laughed at the ridiculously modest gesture, coming after what they'd shared, but she looked so completely, disarmingly alluring. Looking at her made his stomach tighten, and he knew, even if he had the rest of his life, he'd never tire of being with her.

But Dillon was nothing if not a realist. And, as soft and giving as she'd been, there were things going on in that head of hers that he had to know. He couldn't keep her safe otherwise. Not after what he'd learned.

He sat back against the headboard and pulled her slightly resisting body to his side. "We have to talk," he said with quiet bluntness. He wanted to tell her everything. He owed her that. "Sami, it's time to talk. Don't you think?"

"You go first," she said uneasily.

"All right. But first, I was hoping you'd tell me why you're protecting your father."

She stiffened against him, her eyes wide. "What?" She pulled away, her knuckles white from the grip on his sheets. "What did you just ask me?"

"Are you trying to protect your father?" he asked gently, stroking her arm. He could understand, knew firsthand about family loyalty.

"I'm an idiot." Her color drained. "A complete idiot." She leaped from him in one quick motion, scrambling to the far side of the room. "You—You jerk!" She threw the pillow at him with deadly accuracy, hitting him square on the jaw. Stunned, he stared at her while she asked in a deceptively calm voice, "Is that what this was all about? Getting information? *How dare you.*"

"Now wait a minute." He dodged another pillow and tried to figure out where the hell this conversation had gone bad. He came to his knees in the bed. "You came to me, remember?"

Her shoulders sagged as she stared at him. "Oh,

God. You're right. That makes it worse." She grappled with the pile of discarded clothing, yanking on her sweater with jerky motions while he came toward her. "Don't," she warned, glaring at him. "Don't say a word." His shirt flew across the room, then his pants. "Where's my underwear—Oh, never mind." She thrust one bare leg into her jeans.

The sound of the front door opening startled them both. Their surprised gazes met. Dread filled Dillon. He hadn't told her quickly enough, dammit. Things were getting out of control, and he hated that. He yanked on his jeans, cursing. He ran to the stairs, stopping long enough to send Sami a hard look. "I'll be right back. Stay here. *Please*," he added at the mutinous glare she sent him.

She lifted her chin and looked away. Good enough, he thought.

Less than two minutes later, Dillon stood barefoot in the driveway, watching the car zoom down the drive. The close call had him sweating in the cool sun.

"Who was that?"

Sami's voice, coming from directly behind him, made him flinch. He hadn't realized she'd been standing there, and he hoped, oh, how he hoped, he could explain. Forcing himself to move slowly and easily, he turned, pasting a lazy smile on his face. "Nobody important."

Her eyes narrowed, and she put her hands on her fully dressed hips. A flash of disappointment streaked through him that she didn't still lay damp and sated in his bed.

"Obviously you had plans—it's a holiday after all. I'm sorry if I ruined anything." She turned on her heels and headed toward her car.

"Wait." He reached her in less than two strides and gently turned her around. "Let me explain."

She flung his hands off her, her voice low and furious. "I'm sure you can call her back. Again, I'm sorry."

He was quicker this time and caught her as she spun away. "Sami, would you give me a minute? You've got this all wrong."

She laughed shortly, shading her eyes from the bright sun. She turned her head away, but not before he caught the telling glint of tears shimmering. "Really?" she said, choking them back. "Let's see how wrong I have it. I think you had sex with me to soften me up for more information. To find out if I'm somehow protecting my father—from what I have no idea. Do I have that wrong?"

"Yes!" He curtailed his growing frustration and anger, knowing he had to do this carefully. He had to somehow tell her the entire truth and hope she'd forgive him for what he'd done. "You have that *very* wrong." He slid his hands up and down her chilled arms, alarmed at her color, at the hurt in her eyes. He'd done that to her, he thought with disgust. "Please, Sami. Come back inside. We'll talk."

"No." She shrugged off his arm and pulled out her keys. "I want to go."

"You can't. Not until we straighten this out."

The flash of fear in her eyes froze him. Damn her, after all this time she could still fear him, could still believe the worst of him.

"I'll go if I want." Her voice shook. "Move, please."

He wouldn't physically restrain her. That would only make the barrier between them all that much stronger. She ducked around him and ran to her car. She fumbled with her lock, her fingers trembling. He reached around her and steadied her hand. "Let me—"

"No." She gave up and dropped her head on her arms on the top of the car. "Just . . . leave me alone."

"I can't." He touched her shoulder, swept his hand over her back. "Who hurt you?" She went absolutely still. "I can't stand to have you be afraid of me," he said softly. She didn't so much as breathe. "I'd never hurt you, Sami. Never."

She turned her head to look at him. "You have a temper," she said cautiously.

"Yeah, I do." He stroked her hair. "I like to shout. I like everyone to know when I'm angry. But I can be mad as hell and never hurt you, Sami. I swear it." She blinked and remained silent. "Tell me who did."

"No one." She chewed her cheek. "Not for a long time anyway."

"Tell me."

She closed her eyes. "It's silly. It happened ages ago. My mother had this boyfriend. I was eight. And he . . ."

She hesitated, and his stomach tightened. "He what?"

"He liked to hurt me."

He hadn't thought he could feel such fury, certainly had never before felt the urge to kill.

"I was too afraid to tell, at first. Even when the marks would show, I'd lie about how I got them."

God, she'd been just a baby. How could someone hurt a sweet, innocent little girl? How could her mother allow it? With the rage suffocating him, he forced a deep breath. "What happened?"

"Eventually I learned love doesn't have to hurt." She lifted her chin. "I may be a little gun-shy with men, Dillon. But I'm not stupid. Just because we had sex doesn't mean we're obliged to tell all."

There was that prissy tone again she used as a defense. "No, it doesn't." He looked in her nervous eyes. "I hate what happened to you when you were young, Sami. But I'm glad you told me, it explains a lot." He held her face when she would have looked away. "But what happened upstairs wasn't sex. We made love, and we did it because we both wanted to." He moved closer, yearning. "You should know, it's never been like that for me before. Never." She didn't speak, didn't move. "I only brought up your father because I wanted to clear the air between us, once and for all. No more secrets, Sami. I'll come clean and so will you."

She slid in her car. "I was a fool today," she whispered, turning on the car. "It's not your fault. I'm sorry."

"Sami, don't go. Please."

She released the brake. "I'm sorry," she said again. "Just let me go."

How could he when she had this invisible tie on his heart? Yet he had to. He watched her drive away, an unbearably heavy ache in his chest.

He loved her.

Without a doubt, he loved her. He knew they could work it out, if she'd only let them.

❖━━━━━━❖

Sami refused herself the luxury of thinking of Dillon as she sent her car skimming over the slick highway toward the airport. She knew from the flight schedule she'd viewed the night before that Clark had requested an early arrival time. Since her policy was to adjust Reed's hours with enough advance notice, she had reluctantly given the okay for a line crew to come in one hour early. She refused to make a statement by changing the rules for him and denying his request. Besides, he needed a major maintenance service, money she could ill afford to turn away.

The line crew wouldn't go to waste. Dillon, too, had an early flight. He'd appreciate the extra help. The crew could pull out his plane for him with the tug, saving him from having to operate what he called "the ancient machine" himself. Not that it mattered to her what he thought.

Right. She sighed. She'd take the credit for placing herself in the stupid position of being alone with a man she couldn't resist. But that he'd had an ulterior motive to what had happened really hurt. And for the thousandth time since he'd said so three days earlier, she wondered what he'd meant by accusing her of protecting her father.

She pulled into the airport with ten minutes to spare and was shocked to find the place empty. No line crew. She cursed to herself as she ran through the lobby, unlocking the doors and flipping lights on as she went. Pushing the switch to raise the huge hangar doors, she watched as the noisy door lifted, sunlight filled the inside.

She dashed into the head lineman's office and grabbed the tug's key. If Clark came before her crew, she would have to operate the tug to pull his plane into the maintenance hangar.

Out of breath now, she ran into maintenance, heels echoing noisily, where she would have to pull out the tug and drive it down the airstrip several hundred yards to wait for Clark's arrival. She called air traffic control to confirm the flight. Three minutes out. Damn. She intercommed line crew. Nothing. Panting from exertion, she awkwardly hauled herself up into the tug's driver's seat.

"What the hell do you think you're doing?"

She jumped at the sight of Dillon standing in front of the tug, legs planted firmly apart, hands on his hips, the fiercest frown she'd ever seen in place. Her heart gave a little treacherous leap.

"I asked you what you think you're doing."

"What does it look like?" She blew a stray hair out of her face, irked at her breathlessness, which she assured herself came from the running around she'd done, nothing else. "Move. There's a flight coming in."

"Get down."

She turned on the tug, giving him a smug little smile. It started cantankerously, sputtering to life with a loud roar. "You'd better move," she shouted over the din.

He most likely cursed then. She had no way of knowing for sure, since she couldn't hear anything over the tug, but by the dark look he sent her and the way his lips moved, she was sure it wasn't good-morning banalities. She revved the engine warningly.

"Let me do it," he yelled.

He didn't think she could do it. "Move."

"Come on, Sami. You can't drive a tug dressed like that."

It helped her mood to be mean. "Move, or you'll be scraping yourself off the floor."

He moved so quickly, she didn't have time to react. He scooped her off the seat and dumped her—luckily on her feet—next to the tug. He sat in the driver's seat before she could even open her mouth.

"What do you think you're doing?"

His smile disappeared. "I'm trying to help you, Sami. Let me be a nice guy."

"But you're not."

"You could give me a chance," he said solemnly. "I'm really not so bad. You didn't return any of my phone calls this weekend."

"No." She . . . couldn't.

"I came by twice."

"I've been busy. You're in my tug, Dillon."

"What were you going to do with it?"

"There's a flight coming in any second. It needs to be towed to maintenance."

He saluted her and hit the gas. She stepped out of the hangar into the early sunlight, shielding her eyes from the glare, watching as the tug slowed to a halt at the runway. Clark's plane had just landed and it slowly approached. Even from one hundred yards away she could distinguish the tall, broad frame of Dillon.

He hadn't gloated over Thanksgiving and how she'd thrown herself at him. That wasn't fair, she thought. He wouldn't. So why was she still so angry? Pride, she guessed. She'd wanted so badly to believe he'd wanted to be with her as much as she'd wanted to be with him.

When she looked again, Dillon was maneuvering the large plane into the hangar. The new jet dwarfed her as it moved slowly past. Dillon pulled straight in, Clark's new multimillion-dollar prized jet giving him plenty of momentum. As he reached the far wall, Sami waited for him to slow.

He didn't.

With a shout of surprise, Dillon stomped with both feet on the brake, practically standing on the pedal.

Still, the jet didn't slow.

They moved far too quickly toward the inside metal wall of the maintenance hangar, and there was nothing she could do but watch in growing horror at the speed of the tug with the huge plane behind it. She could tell by the set of Dillon's shoulders and the way he fought the steering and the brakes that something had gone very, very wrong.

They came within twenty feet of the wall, the tug with the plane directly behind it, and still didn't slow. Dillon stood and threw his weight into the steering, yanking hard to the right, his every muscle straining. The tug slowed slightly and turned, but not nearly enough to clear the wall.

Ten feet left. The wall loomed large before Dillon—and tons of steel with momentum behind him, waiting to crush him between the two.

"Dillon!" Sami screamed, picturing him smashing into the wall a split second before the enormous jet crashed in directly after him.

ELEVEN

Dillon yanked harder on the steering wheel, every muscle and bone in his body straining painfully as he worked frantically to avoid a collision. A quick glance over his shoulder at the huge nose of the jet immediately behind him had him renewing his efforts with desperate haste. The tug lumbered into the turn, finally responding, and slowly ran out of momentum, coming to a stop a foot from the side wall.

Sami ran into the hangar, skidding to a stop by the tug to suck in her breath. He knew what she was thinking as she stared in amazement at the wall.

The jet had missed the concrete wall by a scant five inches.

He collapsed into the driver's seat, resting his head on the steering wheel, unable to move a muscle.

Sami reached out to touch him, then changed her mind. She stared at his profile, watching as he gulped in a deep breath of air. A trickle of sweat ran down his neck. "Dillon."

He raised his head and pierced her with a look of rage. "No brakes."

She nodded, swallowing her fear for him. "Are you all right?"

"Who messed with the brakes, Sami?"

"I—" Had she ever seen such glowering rage? "I don't know."

He made a sound of disgust and threw himself out of the tug. "You could have been the one. You know that?"

She had just assimilated the fact that he wasn't mad at her, but *for* her. He knew, better than she, the strength it had taken to avoid a collision. At best, she would have destroyed another of Clark's planes. The worst didn't bear thinking about.

"God, Sami." The anger seemed to drain out of him, and he took her shoulders in hands that trembled. Thinking he needed comfort after his near miss, Sami allowed him to pull her close. Without hesitation, she wrapped her arms around his waist, resting her cheek against the fierce pounding of his heart.

"You could have been killed," he whispered gruffly against her hair, his arms tightening around her. "That jet would have killed you."

She pulled back to stare into his green eyes, which had darkened with worry, fright, and anger. "Luckily, I wasn't the one driving."

His jaw tightened. "Luck had nothing to do with this. God, don't you get it? First the shelves falling, then the plane crashing through the office, and now this." She stared at him with growing horror, and he ran a shaky hand over his face. "Someone's trying to hurt you."

"This was an accident. That tug hasn't worked properly in years."

"Okay, Sami. Let's check into the real world here." He grabbed her wrist and started to pull her along with him. "We need to talk and we're going to do it now. We should have done it a long time ago, certainly on Thanksgiving, but what the hell."

"You've got a plane in here that needs work?" Ricardo called out, Clark right behind him. He stopped abruptly, staring at the very unusual parking job of the jet, jackknifed with the tug. He divided an inquisitive look between Dillon and Sami. "Is this what it looks like?"

"Yes," Dillon said tersely, still pulling Sami toward the door. "Save the brake line for me. I think you'll find it's been cut." On that shocking statement, he led Sami firmly out of the hangar.

"What's going on?" Dillon demanded of Sami the minute her office door shut behind them.

"I don't know."

He was sick that the next time he wouldn't be around to help her. "Why didn't you tell me it was Clark's plane I was going to be moving?"

Sami shut a file drawer and turned to him, her arms crossed. She didn't trust him, and the fact that he couldn't make her terrified him. "This is no time to go mute on me. Someone's after you, and we've got to figure out who. Clark? Your father? *Who?*"

She bit her lower lip in a gesture so utterly vulnerable and feminine that he wanted to go wrap his arms around her and never let go. "Fine." He sighed. "You don't like me. Hell, I can understand that. But you've got to believe me on this one. I'm the only one you can trust right now. Please, Sami. Trust me." Knowing he didn't deserve it didn't help.

She looked at him where he leaned against her desk. "I don't know who to trust." She shivered and walked past him, her arms wrapped around herself.

He reached out and caught her, pulling her slowly and gently toward him, settling her between his thighs. "Sami, about what happened between us this weekend—"

"Don't. I don't want to talk about it," she whispered, her breath catching in her throat, reminding him of the sexy, little helpless sounds she'd made when they'd made love. It didn't matter how serious the situation was, his body tightened in remembered response.

"It was special, Sami. It felt incredibly right to be with you. . . . Oh, yeah, I want to talk about it with you a lot. But *this* has to come first. Your safety has to come first."

"You're hiding things from me, Dillon."

He'd planned on telling her about Kevin. About what had happened to him the night before she'd come to see him. But now it seemed too dangerous for her to know.

They stared miserably at each other. Then Sami glanced down at her clenched fists. Her breath caught again, her gaze riveted to the center of his trousers, where he was painfully erect. Her expressive eyes lifted to his.

"I can't help it," he whispered, bracketing her jaw with one hand. "I want you."

"You already had me," she said without rancor.

"It wasn't enough. It could never be enough." She looked away, and he sighed. This wasn't the time to tell her he couldn't picture his life without her. She'd need time, convincing. He cupped her face. "Nothing's changed for me, Sami. I wanted you then, and I want you now. More if possible."

She stared at him.

"Look, I'm not sorry about what happened between us. What I am sorry for is my bad timing. It led you into thinking I had ulterior motives and that isn't so. Okay?"

She hesitated, then leaned into him a little. The fist around his heart loosened. "Okay."

"Sami," Lucy's voice said over the intercom. "You won't believe it. There was no early morning shift scheduled for today."

Sami turned to him when Lucy clicked off. The fear he'd seen after he'd stopped the tug was back in her eyes. "It looks like someone changed the schedule on me," she said.

"So that you'd be the only one here."

"And I'd be forced to use the tug myself. Only they didn't count on your gallantry."

He ignored her sarcasm. "A heavy steel shelf that's been in place for years came tumbling down for no reason. A plane crashes through an office window. Now this. You're near them all. Too many coincidences, Sami. Too damned many." She wouldn't look at him. "Okay," he said in a deceptively calm voice. "You asked for it, you're going to get it."

Fear flared inside her. She stepped back and crossed her arms.

"No, damn you." He nearly shook her. "Don't you

ever be afraid of me. I'm talking about trust, Sami. I must be crazy, but I'm going to tell you." To get her to trust him, he'd have to trust her first.

"What are you talking about?"

He lowered her into a chair, then squatted before her, holding her hands. "Kevin is my brother."

She opened her mouth. She stared at him. She closed her mouth. "Your brother."

"Yes. I'm not here to run Kinley Charters. It's a front for my investigation of his accident."

"I knew it," she said quietly. "I knew something was different about you." She looked at him, studied his face. "You look alike." She shook her head. "But Kevin's last name is Scott."

"No, that's his middle name. He never uses his last."

"Why didn't you just tell me who you are?"

"Because," he said as gently as he could, "the circumstances surrounding his accident stink. And I think you know it." He debated telling her the rest, telling her what he'd learned the night before she'd shown up on his doorstep, but that part could wait for now.

She stood abruptly, brushing past him. "You lied to me from the beginning. You never even gave me the benefit of the doubt, Dillon. Even after we'd . . . become friends, you still lied."

His gut twisted at the hurt and betrayal he'd inflicted. It ached even more when he realized how much more hurt she was going to get before this thing was over. "I didn't know I could trust you then."

A myriad of emotions ran over her face as she looked at him. "And now?"

What would she say if she knew he'd told her only

half the truth? That the other half would change every-thing? How did he tell the most important person in his life he couldn't trust her with the entire truth—for her own sake?

"Well," she said quietly, with a great deal of dig-nity. "I guess that about says it all. Doesn't it?" She moved to the door.

"And now," he said, stopping her and taking her hands in his. "I trust you. With my life."

Her expression softened slightly, and she squeezed his hands softly. "I'm so sorry, Dillon."

"About what?"

"About Kevin. I'm so sorry about your brother."

"I'll be right back," Dillon said to Sami late that night in his office. He didn't want her out of his sight. "Don't—"

"Yeah, yeah." She waved him out, sipping her hot chocolate from her perch near his desk where she'd been working. Her heels had long been kicked off, her stocking feet tucked beneath her. She'd peeled off her jacket hours ago, leaving a pale silk blouse she'd yanked from her skirt for comfort. It clung to her every curve, leaving Dillon capable of little thought except dream-ing about what lay underneath it. And if he felt ob-sessed, he could only imagine what the person stalking her felt.

"I mean it, Sami. I don't want you to—"

"I know, I know." She mocked him with a sweet smile. "Don't go anywhere, don't pick up the phone, don't even move. Oh yeah, and don't breathe until you get back. Do I have it right?"

He grinned. "Yeah, you got that right, smart-ass. I'll be right back." He hated leaving her alone, for even a second, but it had to be done. He'd canceled his flights for the day and stuck to her side, much to her amusement. Now they were alone in the deserted airport because she'd stubbornly insisted she had work to do. He'd had no choice but to stay with her. He intended to stay with her until this entire mess was over.

He needed to use the phone, but couldn't risk Sami hearing him. The only thing he could think of was the pay phone outside the lobby. He'd gotten across the hangar and was reaching for the lobby door when he heard her scream, high-pitched and full of terror. He was running full speed back to his office, pulling out his gun when the second scream came.

Sami watched Dillon leave the office. He was worried, and now so was she. Someone, and she didn't want to think who, wanted to either hurt her or scare the daylights out of her. It was working.

It could be Clark. Okay, the man was a creep, but without her, Reed Aviation would be closed. He couldn't possibly benefit from that. It could be her father, but she couldn't believe that either. Even in the coldest of terms, he needed her.

When the door to the office opened less than a minute later, she raised her head in surprise. She heard a heavy thud, then caught a glimpse of a tall figure crumpling to the ground.

She leaped to her feet, staring at the collapsed body, then in fright at the empty doorway. She slunk back against the wall and crouched down next to a filing cabinet with her heart in her throat, wondering where the attacker was. And who lay on the floor.

Where was Dillon?

Through the open doorway, a shadow moved on the wall. She made out the shape of an arm, raising, extended over a head, holding something long.

She screamed before she could stop herself.

The shadow straightened suddenly and vanished. Sami, one hand held firmly over her mouth, her breath coming in short puffs, stood unsteadily. She raced to the fallen figure and gingerly turned him over.

Then, for the first time in her life, she fainted.

Dillon dropped to his knees next to where Sami lay in a small heap on the concrete floor. He tucked his gun away and ran his hands up and down her limbs, trying to figure out how she was injured. She moaned, and he lifted her against him. "Sami?"

Her eyes opened, dazed and unfocused. She saw him and flung herself against his chest, nearly knocking them both over. He held her violently shaking body close. "What, Sami? What is it?" He smoothed back her hair, frowning at her cool, sticky skin. "You must have fainted. You look like you've seen a ghost." She whimpered and clutched at him.

"She did."

Dillon looked over his shoulder to the chair behind the desk. Kevin sat in it, holding his head, where already, a bluish-purple bruise had developed. But basically, he still looked as cocky, mischievous, and boyishly cute as ever.

He shot his beloved brother an annoyed look then

forced a soothing smile on his face as he tilted his head down to Sami's. "It's all right, Sami." He sighed heavily when she continued to tremble. "I guess it's time I told you the rest of the story. About who stopped in the night before Thanksgiving." He gave his brother another look and put her gently into a chair.

Sami didn't take her eyes off his brother. The minute he set her down, she straightened. "Kevin?"

He smiled, then winced, holding his head. "Ouch. Yeah, it's me. I'm sorry I scared you."

"You were hit! I saw the shadow." She whirled to Dillon. "There was someone else in the hallway."

"They're long gone now." Kevin gingerly felt the swelling bump on his head.

"You're alive." Sami stared at the gun Dillon had tucked into his pants. "Somebody," she said shakily. "Tell me what's going on."

Dillon and Kevin exchanged a long, telling look. "You okay?" Dillon asked him.

"Yeah. I've got a hard head." He grinned suddenly, then just as quickly winced. "Ouch, dammit. I solved our little case."

"Good."

"*Now*," she said with a firm and calm voice that didn't fool Dillon. "Somebody tell me what's going on *now*."

"Sami," he said gently. "Kevin never died in that accident."

"He never died."

"I faked my death so that I couldn't be framed for a crime I didn't commit," Kevin added helpfully. "I—"

"You didn't die," she repeated slowly.

"No. I—"

"Did you know he wasn't dead?" she demanded of Dillon, looking at him with huge, hurting eyes. "*Did you?*"

"Not until the night before we . . . the night before Thanksgiving," he finished lamely as her eyes widened. "I was going to tell—"

She laughed shakily. "You were going to tell me. Exactly when would that have been, Dillon?"

"Sami, listen to me," he said urgently, desperate for her to understand. "This doesn't change anything. Somebody is still trying to hurt you. We've got to—"

"Wrong." She stood up, eyes flashing. He recognized that look, he thought with dread. Pure stubbornness. "*We're* not going to do anything. *You're* going to leave. Take the dead guy here with you."

"Sami—"

"Everything you told me earlier, in my office, was a lie." She paced the room. "You said you trusted me. *With your life.*" He winced at the pain in her voice. "You never did. When did you think you were going to tell me about this? The next time you wanted to sleep with me?"

Kevin straightened in surprise, dividing an amused look between the two.

"Sami—"

"You never planned on telling me at all, did you?"

"No," he admitted tightly, striding toward her. "Not until this mess was over." He had to straighten this out with her now, or he knew he'd lose her. The accusations swimming in her eyes were daunting, but the danger was real. He couldn't risk her running, not now. Gripping her shoulders tight, he said, "It isn't safe here. Obviously, someone saw Kevin. Did you hear that?" He gave her a little shake to be sure. "We're all in danger because of what we know. We could all die if we don't team together here. You don't want that, do you?"

She shook her head, mute.

He gentled his hold. "So let's get out of here, all of us, and we'll go talk. We'll explain everything. Okay?"

She looked at Kevin, who smiled with such a sweet mixture of regret, encouragement, and charm that a monk couldn't have resisted him. "It's going to be okay, Sami. You'll see," he said softly.

"But what happened?" she asked. "Who was going to frame you?"

"It's a long story. But I'll tell you everything if you come with us. Trust me?"

Dillon watched the war rage within her. She pulled away from him and walked up to Kevin, touching the bump on his head gently, then hugged him to her, leaving Dillon in the unusual position of feeling ridiculously jealous of his own brother. "I'm glad you're alive, Kevin," she whispered. "Whatever the reason. I'm so very glad."

His arms went around her tightly. "Me, too, Sami. Me too. Come with us."

"Kevin," Dillon interjected warningly, wishing his brother wasn't looking as if he enjoyed holding Sami so much. "We need to get out of here. Now."

Kevin smirked knowingly over Sami's back. "Save the reunion for later, dammit," Dillon snapped, wondering how long Sami would be mad at him.

Sami glared at him. He wasn't off the hook yet, obviously. "How you're related is beyond me," she said. "Kevin is too sweet and considerate to be your brother."

Nope. He wasn't off the hook. Not by a long shot. The satisfied grin Kevin shot him only further annoyed him. His brother was definitely not helping his case with Sami. "If you're done socializing," he said as calmly as he could manage, "we really need to scram."

Kevin rubbed his head. "No kidding."

"Let's go," Dillon said roughly, his fear compounding his irritability. He grabbed Sami's elbow and pulled her to the door.

Just then, the lights flickered briefly then went out. Complete darkness settled over them, the only light coming from the greenish glow of Kevin's watch. Outside the office door it was pitch-black.

Dillon cursed long and luridly. He should have known. "Kevin, stick to her back." He reached for his gun. "We'll be fine," he whispered to Sami. "Don't worry."

"I forgot," she hissed in the darkness. "I'm with the master of all trades. Let me guess, you're an undercover cop. No, scratch that. You're an FAA investigator. No, that wouldn't fit either. You lie too much for that particular occupation. Maybe you're a—"

The air whooshed out of her as he grabbed her close and squeezed her tight against him. "Quiet, Sami," he whispered warningly in her ear. "Or you'll get us killed yet." She went still, but he could nearly taste her fury.

The hallway was long. They could see nothing, not even their own hands in front of their faces. Even Dillon, who had the security of a gun in his hand, didn't relish the thought of walking down it. They'd be sitting ducks. They had to get through the hangar, then the lobby—both equally dark and equally dangerous.

They maneuvered themselves wordlessly down the hall, side by side with Sami in the middle. A few feet short of where Dillon estimated the opening to the hangar to be, he paused. He'd heard a noise. He backed them up a few steps, and they waited silently.

Three minutes passed. An unendurably long time when one is standing rod-stiff and still, but then the soft scuffle came again. Dillon imagined someone navigating through the dark by shuffling his feet, arms outstretched.

Suddenly, Kevin's hand ripped from his and a loud crash of metal hitting metal rent the air.

"Oh, hell," Kevin muttered, his voice sounding muffled.

"What happened?" Dillon whispered.

"I tripped over something. A chair, I think."

"Oh, Kevin," Sami whispered, dropping down and feeling for him. "Are you okay?"

Listening to her fuss over his clumsy brother like a worried mother hen when a nameless someone behind them was possibly trying to kill them was too much. "Jesus!" he exploded in a raging whisper. "Now that you've announced our whereabouts, can we get on with it?"

An unmistakable ping of a bullet ricocheted off the walls, bringing them quickly to their senses. Kevin remained on the ground while Dillon flew himself at where he'd last heard Sami's voice. He tackled her to the floor and covered her with his body.

TWELVE

Dillon threw himself over her, smacking her chin on the concrete, rattling her teeth and knocking the air from her. Her next thought, as a second bullet bounced over their heads, was that they needed to get the hell out of there. Fast.

"There's a door to the airstrip beyond the line crew's office," she whispered as softly as she could. She felt Dillon nod and move off her. He covered her from behind as she crawled forward, holding Kevin's hand.

They reached the door safely and ran down the airstrip in the cold night air, then around the hangar and to the parking lot. They stared at one another in anticlimactic shock.

Dillon shoved her inside his Jeep, keeping a surveying eye on their surroundings. The minute they were all in, he hit the gas, getting as much distance as possible between them and whoever followed them. He dialed the sheriff on his car phone, reporting the break-in.

"They'll find nothing," Kevin said wearily.

"What were you, before you came to Bear Pass?" Sami asked Dillon. "A cop?"

Kevin snickered. "No," Dillon said.

"What then?"

"I started out as an Air Force pilot."

"And then?" she pressed.

"I had a special . . . knack for covert operations." His voice was heavy with irony. "I ended up as sort of a special agent."

"Doing what?" She imagined all sorts of dangerous things.

He frowned. "Leave it alone, Sami. It's over. That part of my life is over."

They kept a terse silence. In the backseat, Kevin closed his eyes, looking bedraggled and a little gray around the edges. His breath still heaved from their run to the car. She couldn't seem to catch hers either.

Dillon's face looked tense, his eyes hard and aware. But despite their struggle and near escape, he wasn't even remotely winded. It made her more angry. "What were you doing carrying a gun?"

He kept his eyes on the slick road. "Saw that, did you?"

"*Why* Dillon?"

"I thought it might come in handy."

"Would you have used it?"

He glanced at her. "If I had to," he said finally, his steady green gaze returning to the road.

He would have protected his brother and her with a gun. The thought stunned her. It said a lot about the man. It unsettled her to know yet another layer had peeled away.

"Did you send me the letters?"

"No."

"Who did, Dillon?"

"Not me, okay?" His voice softened, and he sighed loudly. "I was as shocked as you were."

"I sent them," Kevin said from the backseat, his eyes still closed. "Dillon was furious when he found out, but I was worried about the risks you were taking."

Dillon said nothing, didn't attempt to apologize for his part in the entire ruse. She closed her eyes on the humiliation. She'd thrown herself at that man's feet—and his bed—thinking there was something between them. There'd never been anything, nothing except his need to do whatever it took to protect his brother.

She had no idea where Dillon intended to take them until Dillon pulled up before her condo. "I don't have keys," she said. "And I never put my spare set back out."

He slanted her a look. "You know as well as I do that you have a code to bypass the thing. What is it?"

She told him, annoyed she couldn't rattle his calm. Then, to her surprise, Dillon broke effortlessly into her condo, and they stood in her living room.

"I feel as if I don't know you," she said, staring at him.

He made a sound of protest and touched her face. Why did her heart leap like that at his touch? It really wasn't fair that for the first time in her life she felt so much for a man who'd never been honest with her.

It seemed like eons since she'd been home. Her answering machine's light blinked incessantly. She sighed and walked toward it.

Kevin looked at Dillon. "You came just in time tonight."

"Almost too damned late," Dillon said, disgust welling up inside him. "Again."

"Dillon, I didn't die. Remember?"

"No thanks to me." Dillon sank wearily to the couch. "God, Kev, every time I think about what you went through—"

"It's over," Kevin said. "And we're together. Are you going to leave again, when this is all over?"

He saw the resignation in his brother's eyes. "No," Dillon said quietly, never more sure of a decision in his life. "How does a partnership sound to you?"

"In the charter?" Kevin's eyes lit. "Sounds good. Real good." He glanced at Sami across the room, listening to her messages. He said, looking thoughtful, "You never told me that you two, ah . . . well, you know." Dillon shifted uncomfortably, and Kevin smiled knowingly. "That's who was over on Thanksgiving. Geez, the way you kicked me out, I should have known." His amusement faded to a sudden frown. "You know she's different. She doesn't deserve to be just another of Dillon Kinley's women."

"Did it ever occur to you," Dillon asked tightly, "that maybe *she* won't be the one to get hurt?"

Kevin stared at him and then laughed softly. "Oh, man. She got you, didn't she? She really got you." He laughed again and then scrunched up his face, holding his head.

Sami turned to them from across the room, and they both rose at her frightened, pale expression. She pushed the button on her machine and turned up the volume.

"Samantha," her father's strangely weakened and gruff voice echoed throughout the room. "I was released from the hospital today. But I . . . I fell ill again. I'm at Bakersfield Community Hospital." There was a long, pregnant pause. "Please come."

"Why Bakersfield, Sami?" Dillon asked into the silence of the Jeep as he drove her to the hospital.

"My mother is buried there." Her father must have gone to her grave, a statement if he'd ever made one. "He must be very sick."

"You look pale."

"I hardly ever look my best while being hunted down by an unknown madman with a gun and being escorted by two brothers—one of whom I thought was dead, and the other I thought . . . well, never mind what I thought."

He risked another long look at her, his expression holding a sweet regret that seemed sincere enough to make her pulse trip. "This entire thing—Kinley Charters, you a tenant, it was all a ruse. A scam to get information. Right?"

His knuckles whitened at the steering wheel from his grip. "Yes. But—"

"Don't!" She couldn't take another lie, another farce.

The Jeep swerved sharply and jerked to a stop. He gripped her shoulders, whipping her around to face his fury. "That's how it started, yes. I came for Kevin's sake. He asked me for help, dammit, and it took me two months to respond."

She could see he blamed himself. The hard ball of

betrayal and anger dissolved. "You must have had a good reason," she said slowly.

Her unquestioning faith in him stunned him. "Not good enough." He pounded the steering wheel. "I thought he was dead, Sami. *Dead.* You should know how that felt. I had to do something, anything, to make myself feel better. I dreamed of revenge. But then I met you, and I started to care for you. I put you in danger. I hate knowing that."

Those eyes could make her believe anything. He slid his long, taut body closer, until all she could concentrate on was his proximity, his hard thigh pressing hers, his dark, intent expression running over her face. Soothing warm fingers spanned her neck from chin to collarbone. His touch left her restless for more, her mind treacherously drawing images of his strong hands on her body, coaxing responses from her that no one else ever had.

"I never meant to hurt you," he said quietly, his thumb dragging a sensuous path across her lower lip. It tingled, yearning for a kiss. "And I never, ever meant for you to get caught up in this mess. But now you are, and I can't let anything happen to you."

"Because you'll feel guilty. The way you did over Kevin." Her lower lip glanced across the tip of his thumb as she spoke.

His eyes darkened, and she closed hers against an onslaught of unspeakable need. She wanted to be held, loved, assured by him. When her eyes opened again, he'd moved closer. "It's much, much more than that," he murmured. "You've become very important to me."

"Did you plan to leave when this was all over?"

"Yes," he admitted. "At first. But things changed. Would that be so hard to believe?"

She wanted to believe, oh, how she wanted that. But she needed to think. It started to rain.

"I see it would." He sounded disappointed. "I'll just have to prove it to you."

He threw the Jeep into gear, and they traveled the rest of the long, wet ride in silence.

By the time they'd pulled into the hospital parking lot nearly two hours later, the storm had come upon them with incredible fury. "Let's go before we get stuck here for the night," Dillon said.

"I should have come alone."

"No way," he said. He locked up, even now, miles and miles from Bear Pass, unable to shake the feeling of danger.

They got a surprise at the nurses' station. "I'm sorry," the nurse said, checking her admittance sheet. "We have no Howard Reed."

A wild-goose chase, Dillon thought. "We've been duped, Sami."

"No." She walked toward the row of pay phones on the wall. "He's probably been released. I'll call his house."

"Do that," he said, following her, understanding Howard had gotten them—again. "Ask him what Viewmont was doing every one of those nights he flew in at the stroke of midnight without a ground crew. And while you're at it, ask him what's going on that he'd risk his own daughter's life."

She whirled, staring at him, the phone limp in her hand. He expected a fight and braced himself. "You're right, of course," she said, her shoulders square. "It's time."

He moved close, slipped an arm around her waist. "I'll be right here, Sami."

Reed didn't answer, if he was home. "Let's go," Dillon suggested gently. "It's late." He knew Kevin was waiting for them to make their next move—their final move, he corrected. It would all be over in a matter of hours now.

But fate intervened.

They hadn't gotten out of the parking lot when the radio disc jockey informed them the pass had been closed due to heavily falling snow.

Sami seemed stiff, cold, and exhausted—and drained of hope. He intended to change that. He touched her cheek, tucked her wet hair behind her ear. "Let's find a place to stay. We'll talk. No interruptions. No lies. Just you and me and the truth."

She looked at him warily. "There's so much I need to know," she said. "I don't want any more lies."

"I promise." He kept his hand on her face because he had to touch her.

She looked uncomfortable. "My purse is back in my office. I have no money."

He'd been locked in an elevator with her. He'd made love with her. He'd run for their very lives with her, and she was worried about money. A slow grin grew across his face, and with one finger he traced her jawbone. "Yeah? So you're at my mercy."

"I suppose you enjoy that."

He laughed. "Oh, yeah. Very much."

She rolled her eyes and looked away, but she didn't show a spark of real temper. She was probably too tired, but he took heart anyway. "Does that mean you'll come willingly?"

She shrugged. "What choice do I have?"

"Just checking. I hate the thought of dragging you kicking and screaming into some cheap motel. To have you come eagerly will be much better for my image."

She shook her head and closed her eyes. "I said I'd go. I didn't say I'd be *eager.*"

He laughed again.

It wasn't some cheap motel at all, but a Hilton. "Dillon, I don't think this is a good idea." He touched her hand softly, his eyes lit with a tenderness she'd never seen before.

"Do us both a favor, Sami," he said gently. "Just for a little while, don't think."

She was left to her own bleak thoughts while he signed in. Her father had lied. Kevin was alive. Someone wanted her dead. And she was falling hopelessly for a man she knew would break her heart. A hand touched her shoulder and she jumped.

"Just me," Dillon said softly. He took her to a room on the eighth floor.

"What are you doing?" she asked as he shrugged out of his wet jacket.

"Taking off my wet things."

"Oh no," she said firmly, taking a step back and coming in contact with the door. "I'm not sharing a room with you."

He sighed the sigh of a man short on patience. "I can't leave you alone in a hotel room in the middle of nowhere."

She looked at him with all the pent-up resentment she felt, wishing things were different. Wishing he'd come to her and tell her . . . what exactly, she had no idea. "No one knows we're here."

"Your father knows. He sent us."

"You think he's responsible for everything." Her shoulders sagged against the door. She placed her palms flat on it for support.

He stared at her, grim. "Sami." He came toward her.

"No. Wait a minute. I need to think. I annoy my father over the money I spent on renovations for Reed, and a steel shelving unit nearly slices me in half. I won't comply to his wishes about Clark, and a plane crashed into the office where I'm sitting. We have a disagreement, and the tug I'm slated to drive loses its brakes."

Dillon took another step toward her, alarm and concern registering quite clearly.

"Then there's the insane person chasing me down dark hallways with a gun." A sob escaped her, and she threw a hand up to cover her mouth.

Dillon moved the rest of the way to her in an instant, wrapping his warm, strong arms around her. "You're safe here."

She buried her face in his neck and let his already wet shirt soak up her tears. The way he cupped her head to his chest, soothing her, murmuring softly in her ear wasn't in any way sexual, but so completely comforting. She didn't want to be mad at him anymore, she just wanted to be with him.

She pressed closer, seeking warmth against the chill that had invaded her body from the inside out. She knew the exact second the embrace changed. Held to him from head to toe, her body suddenly hummed and vibrated with a sexual awareness.

Startled, she raised her head, staring into his face. She could feel the solid muscles beneath his shirt. She could feel the heat, the desire that emanated from his rigid body. He no longer offered simple comfort, but something much more complicated. He waited.

For her, there was no choice. She wanted him. She always had. Her lips brushed softly over his. She tipped her middle up, bringing her hips to his, thrilling to the low sound he made deep in his throat. She pulled back because she had to see his eyes, and was overwhelmed at the emotion she read there. He cupped her face and kissed her again, a kiss as wild as the storm outside. She arched against him, mindless of everything but this moment, this basic, driving need she had to give in to.

"I want you," he told her. "But I want all of you this time, mind, body, and soul." His hands ran over her, pinning her to him as he pressed a hot, open-mouthed kiss to her throat.

He moved her into the bathroom, letting go of her only long enough to crank on the hot water in the shower. Framing her head in his large hands, he devoured her mouth with his hungry lips. She eagerly returned the reckless kisses, welcoming the drugging inner heat that came with desire.

The room steamed around them, and he slowly peeled off her wet clothes. She did the same for him, enjoying every part of his lean, tough, rugged body. She found scars she hadn't had time to notice before. A warrior, she thought. Her warrior. A little rough around the edges, but real and full of life.

Finally, they stood in the hot, healing water together, and he pulled her to him. "There's so much I want to say to you," he said huskily.

"Just kiss me," she whispered. "Please, just love me." She froze then. *Kiss me*, she'd meant.

"I will," he promised. His eyes closed as his lips roamed her face, and she had no idea if he knew what he'd just promised. His hands squeezed her hips gently, then worked their way upward, building an almost unbearable pressure. The water pounded their weary bodies, invigorating them. "So soft," he whispered, tasting her jaw, her neck, behind her ear as the water ran over them. "So sweet." His fingers splayed wide as they traced her waist, drawing a path over her ribs to the underside of her aching breasts, driving her crazy.

"Dillon." She moved restlessly against him, eager for the mindless passion she knew he could give her. "Touch me."

His hands cupped her breasts, and her thoughts scattered into a thousand pieces like the storm that raged outside. She arched against his fingers as they slid over her, back and forth over the tightened tips until she moaned into his mouth.

She wanted him inside her. "Dillon," she urged, pressing him against her, trying to bring him closer to the spot where she ached so unbearably. "Now. Please. . . ." But he only continued to tease, torment. She streaked her hands down his body, touching him, then encircling him in her hands.

He sucked in his breath sharply, then moaned when she stroked him. "Now," she demanded. "For God's sake, now."

He lifted her thighs and, using the wall behind her as leverage, entered her with one quick, hard thrust.

She cried out and held on, mesmerized by his hot, hard gaze. When she wrapped her legs around his waist, he dragged his lips from hers and said her name on a torn breath.

He didn't move.

Steam surrounded them, warm water rushed over them in waves, making every muscle, every nerve come alive. The tension built in her just from looking at him, feeling him thick and hard inside her. A devastating orgasm barreled through her, leaving her gasping and limp.

He waited until she could breathe again before he moved, slowly at first, increasing the tempo as the water beat down on them. Alive, she thought, she'd never felt so alive, and incredibly, she exploded around him again, just as he tensed within her and found his own release.

Finally, he sighed and looked at her with feverishly bright eyes through the water that dripped down his face. She clung to him, feeling warm, satisfied. Safe.

Then the water turned tepid. So did her body and her emotions. She had deep feelings for this man. Feelings that she'd never felt before. They terrified her.

"What is it?" he whispered in concern, kissing her.

She shook her head, still intimately joined with him. Her eyes closed, and she sagged against him, physically and mentally exhausted. He studied her silently, then gently released her, letting her legs slide slowly down his.

He settled her into bed without a word, but she felt him watching her carefully. Exhaustion claimed her before he'd pulled the cover up over her.

THIRTEEN

Dillon lay next to Sami, watching her sleep. Everything about her fascinated him. Her integrity, her loyalty, her inner strength. Her capacity to forgive. Her desperate and unacknowledged need for love and affection. He intended to fulfill that need.

He'd wanted to tell her how he felt, but she wouldn't let him. She was afraid of what he made her feel. He'd seen it in her face. When she slowly opened her eyes, he smiled at her. "Better?"

"Yes." She started to push herself up, inadvertently exposing herself to her very tantalizing belly button, then clutched the sheet against her, looking horrified as the reality of their circumstances flooded back to her.

"Sami, I promised never to lie to you again."

She gripped the sheet like a lifeline. "I remember."

"Do you believe me?" He reached out and touched her face gently until she looked at him. "Do you?"

"Yes," she said finally, and he nearly sagged in relief. "But I want you to tell me everything. I know you haven't."

"Good or bad first?"

"Bad," she said uneasily.

"Okay." He sat back, their arms touching. "A year ago Kevin flew Viewmont's plane as a favor to your father. He was a young, inexperienced mechanic, hoping to make a good impression. He did, but being as gullible as he is, he ended up getting himself into something he shouldn't have."

"Which was what?"

"He flew illegal cargo into this country unknowingly, and when he refused to do it again, he was blackmailed, threatened with the police. Kevin believed the threat and continued to fly the illegal cargo. When Viewmont had a scare with the authorities, Kevin was going to be used as a convenient scapegoat."

Her face was carefully blank. "So he staged an accident?"

"It was the only way."

"What was the cargo? Drugs?" She played with the sheet, rubbing it nervously between her fingers.

"Illegal aliens flown from Mexico. People pay enormous amounts of money to come here. The only expense is the fuel. It's a guaranteed high profit. Reed Aviation, being small, doesn't have a customs division. It's also only a few hours from the Mexican border. It was a perfect setup."

"My father was in charge of the operation?"

"Possibly with Clark."

"So Kevin got away and then put you on the job to clear his name?"

"No. Even I didn't know he was alive. He couldn't reach me. I was as surprised as you. The only way for him to be safe was for everyone to think he was dead."

"You think they would have killed him?"

"Eventually, yes." She stiffened, and his heart twisted. "Your father got ill. Probably slowed up the illegal operation. Maybe even stopped it entirely. But Clark didn't stay satisfied. And you weren't so complying, were you?"

She looked at him, her eyes filled with those unshed emotions. "No, I wasn't." She even managed a small smile. "I guess I was quite a hindrance—even after Clark tried to persuade me."

His whole body tensed with a violent protectiveness as he remembered exactly how Clark had tried to persuade her. "I'll never stop thanking Mother Nature for my tail wind that day. I should have been nearly thirty minutes later."

She shuddered. "You're safe now," he said, squeezing her.

She relaxed. "I know." She buried her face in his neck. "But none of this proves my father is trying to kill me. I haven't actually gotten hurt. There's no proof."

"Which is the only reason we haven't called the authorities. While you were asleep I called Kevin. Felicia saw him. She says she'll tell everyone Kevin's alive unless we help her."

"Help her?"

"One of the first families Kevin brought over from Mexico was apparently hers. They paid your father every cent they had for the privilege. Then immigration found them and deported them. Your father must have felt guilty enough to give Felicia a job. Maybe he paid her to keep quiet, I don't know. But now she says it was a setup and she wants her family's money back."

"Why now?"

"Probably because she sniffs a big payoff now."

She slumped out of his arms against the headboard, her look of pure despair eating at him. "And if we don't help her?" she asked.

He looked at her, willing her to understand. He loved her, and he loved his brother. He'd protect them both with his life. "If your father learns Kevin's alive . . ."

He didn't have to finish. "He's as good as dead," she said grimly. She had no problem reading the agony on Dillon's face. "How is this going to be all right, Dillon? How?"

"You believe me," he breathed in relief.

"Yes," she said softly, turning to him, touched beyond belief. "It matters that much?"

"You haven't been paying attention," he chided gently, sitting up. The sheet fell away from him, revealing his magnificent body. But what was even more appealing was how comfortable he was with himself, his sexuality, without being the slightest bit arrogant. He touched her. "It matters very much what you think." His gaze settled on her, lit with something she didn't recognize. "Business is over, Sami. I've told you everything. Except how much I love you."

She started in shock, not expecting the words or the onslaught of emotions they caused. "I—"

"No," he said quickly, hauling her up against him. "Don't say anything. I know you're not ready, that you're scared, but it feels right to me. I want to love you, Sami . . . just let me love you." Her head swam, and she didn't think the feeling was necessarily bad. His finger etched a path from her cheek, down her neck and over her collarbone, drawing the sheet slowly, tantalizingly away from her as it went.

Her heart started a dull, heavy pounding that had nothing to do with her fear of the events of the day. His fingers continued down, over a sensitive nipple. Down, over her quivering stomach, then lower still, finding the slippery warmth between her legs. She arched up.

He gently pushed her back, leaning over her as his fingers evoked a low, shuddery moan from her. "I love the no-nonsense, intelligent woman on the outside," he said silkily as he lowered his lips and nuzzled her belly button. "I love the soft, giving woman on the inside." He pushed her thighs apart, cupped her hips in his hands, and lowered his mouth to her.

She gasped in shock, but he ignored it. His tongue delved in deep, and she nearly bucked off the bed, but he held her, soothing her with his hands even as his lips and tongue devoured her. He quit unexpectedly, and she whimpered shamelessly, her sweaty hands slipping limply from his shoulders. He lifted his head and sent her a devil's smile. "And I especially love the soft, helpless sounds you make when I do this." The tip of his tongue teased her, flicking lightly, then sucking deeply until she writhed beneath him, begging for the release he held just out of her reach.

He gave it to her and she was gripped, staggered by the most powerful, passionate sensations she'd ever experienced.

Gradually, she became aware of the fact that the only sound in the room was her own harsh breathing. Dillon caressed her softly as she came back to her senses, kissing his way up her body lazily, ending at her lips. She tasted the forbidden, musky taste of herself and murmured her pleasure.

"I've never . . . I mean—That was amazing," she said finally, in awe. "I had no idea."

He chuckled. "Good." He settled his body between her thighs, nudging his hips against hers suggestively. He was hard again. "Tired?" he asked with a wicked grin.

"No." She reached for him.

When Dillon and Sami woke up in the morning, the roads were clear. Dillon drove with a haste that bordered on reckless. Sami watched him quietly, knowing he worried about Kevin and wondered what it was like to love and care about a sibling.

Dillon loved her. The knowledge both thrilled and terrified her. Her experience in love was truly limited. She'd loved her mother. She'd thought she loved her father. She'd had one boyfriend nearly five years before that had turned out to be a jerk. She didn't trust her judgment.

Dillon had woven himself into her life, and she knew she didn't want to be without him. Did that mean she loved him?

They were close to her condo when Dillon spoke again. "You're going to be all right?"

He meant, of course, would she be able to help him nail her father and Clark and put them in jail. She turned her head and looked out the window. The San Bernardino mountains seemed so beautiful, especially this time of year. Lightly dusted with snow from the night before, they shone brightly in the early morning sun. They'd be skiing by Christmas.

"Talk to me, Sami."

"Do you know how to ski?"

He sighed and pulled over. "Could you look at me? Please?"

She did, then felt staggered by the amount of love and tenderness swimming in his eyes. "All we have left to do is get solid proof, and this thing is over. According to Kevin, a flight's planned for tonight. We'll be there."

"I know." God, those eyes. How had she ever thought they were cold?

"What then?"

Unexpectedly, her eyes filled. "I know he hasn't been much of a father to me. But I just don't want it to be him."

He hugged her fiercely. "I know, Sami, I know."

Pretending everything was normal was the hardest part. Knowing Dillon had canceled his flights and was around helped. Sami stayed busy. Clark Viewmont stayed ominously scarce. So did her father.

A sharp longing for Dillon hit her, though he was only in the next hangar. She wanted to see that rugged face smile at her, his eyes lit with easy emotion. She wanted to talk to him, hold him . . . tell him she loved him.

She loved him. She tried not to panic.

Afternoon faded away. Her intercom buzzed, and she snagged up the receiver but sagged in disappointment.

"Yes, Ricardo," she said quietly, wishing it'd been Dillon.

"We have a problem," he said quickly. "Someone's broken into hangar three."

"I'll be right there," she promised. She dashed through the lobby, disturbed to see that both Lucy and Felicia had already left. Then she ran down the airstrip with disregard to the cold weather that quickly penetrated her lightweight dress. All that mattered was her mother's plane and how she'd feel if it were damaged or stolen. She stepped into the side door of the hangar, which slammed behind her so quickly, the hem of her dress got caught.

Complete darkness enveloped her. She whirled blindly to the door, ripping her dress in the process, and tried to push it open. It couldn't be budged.

A scream welled up, but she forced it down. She so desperately wanted to live, to see Dillon again. Blinking in the all-consuming darkness, she kicked off her heels so she could go silently, then slunk down the hall, hugging the wall in vivid reminder of the previous night in the other hangar when someone had taken shots at them. If luck stayed on her side, she could make it to the side door.

It didn't.

Halfway down the hall, she heard a noise coming from directly in front of her. She slumped against the wall, struggling to silence her racing heart and panicked breathing. Her fingers touched something smooth—the elevator call button! She pushed it and prayed.

The door slid open, and she used the distraction of the squeaky door to quietly open the adjoining door to the stairway. She took the steps two at a time, thankful she knew her way in the dark.

Her dress kept slipping off her shoulder from where she'd ripped it out of the closed steel door below, and she shoved it impatiently back in place as she climbed. Halfway up, she hesitated. If she went up, not only was it a dead end, she might meet whoever took the elevator. If she went down, she might find he didn't take it.

The decision was made for her.

Slowly, from down below, the door to the stairwell opened. A solitary narrow beam of light shot up the stairs. She ran up the rest of the stairs, yanking open the door. More darkness met her, this time it came with a musty, closed-in feeling that engulfed her until she felt surrounded, overwhelmed by the blackness. She stepped away from the door, feeling as though she'd traversed into another world.

There was no front, no back, no edge of the tangible blackness. And she'd never been so terrified in her life. She forced her feet to take the steps that she knew would move her to the first of the six offices that lined the corridor. It was locked.

Damn, damn, damn. Panic had a taste, she discovered. Bitter, tangy . . . blood from where she'd bitten the inside of her cheek.

From somewhere behind her, she heard a sound. She knew she had to move. She yanked her dress back into place and hurried down the hall. Feeling for the doors she knew lined the wall, she counted. One, two, three. At the last door, she paused, eyes wide. Nothing.

She opened the door, wincing at the creak the hinges emitted. Making a quick about-face in the dark, she rapidly backed up, sliding along the wall to the previous door. When it opened silently, she slid in, nearly hysterical with relief.

She heard the other office door open, the one she had almost gone in, and knew that whoever followed her had assumed she was there. It wouldn't be long until they discovered otherwise. She had to move, paralyzed with fear or not. The creak of that other door closing again echoed eerily down the hall, and she flattened herself against the wall, waiting. Her breath came in short pants, born of sheer terror, but she couldn't control it now. She straightened and started to back up, feeling for the wall to get her bearings.

Then she was grabbed from behind and hauled against a thick, menacing body. She opened her mouth to scream, but a hard, curved hand clamped down cruelly over her mouth and nose, making breathing impossible. The other arm wrapped completely around her, imprisoning her arms to her sides, making her helpless.

She lifted her stocking foot and slammed it down as hard as she could on a boot-covered toe. The hand over her mouth lifted, and Sami gulped in a gasp of precious air, then kicked backward with one foot, aiming for the groin.

She connected.

She was dropped, hard, and without a sound, she took off running, paying no heed to her dress slipping off or to the muffled threats behind her. She wished for the flashlight as she headed for the approximate place she thought the stairs were. She glanced backward. No sounds of a chase. Yet. She whirled and ran directly into a solid, ungiving body. Arms closed around her tightly, and she struggled violently, sobbing in frustration. She aimed a knee for a groin again, but missed and got an inner thigh instead.

"Dammit, Sami," Dillon whispered furiously. "Hold still."

Shock had her going limp, and Dillon, who hadn't expected it, nearly toppled down the stairs with her in his arms. They straightened, and then simultaneously stiffened when the unmistakable tread of footsteps came from above. Sami clutched Dillon in terror.

He grabbed her hand, yanking her hard with him as they ran down the stairs, through the hangar, onto the airstrip. The night had gone dark; thick, low clouds swept across the sky, bringing the threat of more snow. The distance between the buildings suddenly loomed like miles. A painful stitch tore through her side. Directly in front of them, hangar two appeared in the night.

Dillon pushed her into it. The door closed behind them, engulfing them in utter darkness again. He pulled her roughly into his arms and buried his face in her hair. "God, Sami." When his hands came in contact with her bare shoulder and arm, he went still. Violent anger seeped from his pores.

"I'm okay," she whispered, gripping him tight.

"Are you sure?" His voice was an agonizing whisper.

"Thanks to you."

His arms tightened, and he sighed on a ragged breath. "I nearly went out of my mind when I knew he had you."

She clung to him and resisted the urge to fall apart. "How did you know where to find me?"

"I got lucky. I was almost too late." He gave her a

quick, hard kiss that said everything that words couldn't. He froze again. "Dammit, you are hurt. I taste blood."

She could hear the self-recrimination, the fear. "No. I bit my lip."

"Sami—" He pushed away from her suddenly and grabbed her hand again. "He's coming."

The words of love wouldn't wait. "Dillon, wait. I lo—"

He covered her mouth with his hand. "Shhh. He's smart."

She sighed over the lousy timing. "*Who?*"

He didn't answer. They walked along the wall, only too aware of how far they were from safety. Dillon stopped so abruptly, she plowed into the back of him. A door opened. Dillon turned and clenched Sami to him. He pressed his lips to her ear. "He's got a light, probably a gun. Are the planes locked?"

She swallowed hard and shook her head. They crept toward the nearest plane, a beautiful Cessna. At the same time, a steady beam of light spread over the other end of the hangar. It moved slowly, searching them out.

They huddled in the cockpit together, Sami squeezing herself as close to Dillon as she could get, taking some comfort in his size and bulk. They'd get out of this, she thought, pressing her head to his chest. He held her tight, engulfing her in his natural heat. "It's going to be all right," he whispered, and she clung to him, wanting to believe it.

The light came closer. Dillon pulled something from his pocket and flung it. The beam of light whipped toward the sound of a coin falling. Sami gasped in surprise as Dillon flew out of the cockpit and hurtled himself on the bulk behind the light. Both figures dropped heavily to the ground, and the flashlight went sliding across the smooth concrete finish.

He'd risked his life for her. With a courage she didn't know she possessed, Sami jumped out of the plane and ran toward the light. Shaking from both the cold and a fear so deep she could hardly stand, she tried to turn the light on the two struggling figures writhing on the floor. Over and over the two rolled on the floor, each throwing and receiving punches with such increasing velocity, Sami felt sick.

Dillon rolled on top of Ricardo, pinning the larger, more bulky man to the floor. Wearing the most aggressive, hardened expression she'd ever seen, Dillon looked down into Ricardo's eyes. Both panted with exertion.

"You think you're on top of things, don't you Kinley?" came Ricardo's low voice. He bled from the nose and mouth and one eye was nearly swollen shut. "You're a fool."

Dillon's jaw tightened, and a drop of blood from a small cut near his mouth only made him look meaner. "Make a move. Give me an excuse to—"

A deafening shot rang out from behind him.

All eyes turned to a second source of light. A dark shadow stood behind it, but the only thing visible was the tip of a large pistol, pointed directly at Sami. A voice said firmly and coldly, "Get off him, Kinley. Do it now or I'll blow her away."

FOURTEEN

Dillon's eyes never left the tip of the gun as he eased off Ricardo.

"That's a good boy," came the taunting voice, and Dillon jerked with surprise as he recognized it. He looked at Sami. She dropped the flashlight and covered her mouth with her hands, eyes wide with shock. His fault, he thought grimly, as he walked to her. He'd brought this on her. He pulled her close.

Felicia lifted a brow and shot him a nasty smile. "I didn't tell you that you could do that. Back away from her."

He wouldn't have, but Felicia again aimed the gun directly at Sami's bowed head. Real fear gripped him. He squeezed Sami tight once and dropped his arms from her.

"Thanks a lot," Ricardo said to Felicia in disgust, dusting himself off. "What the hell took you so long?" He rubbed his ribs, and Dillon hoped they hurt like hell. His did.

"What's the matter, brother?" Felicia slid admiring eyes over Dillon's body. "Couldn't take him?"

Ricardo shrugged. "He's strong."

"I don't understand," Sami said, looking back and forth between Felicia, still holding the gun trained on her, and Ricardo, who stood shakily next to Dillon, dripping blood and sweat. "You're brother and sister?"

"I thought you were going to handle her," Felicia said to Ricardo.

"Well, I wasn't expecting her guardian angel."

Felicia glanced at Dillon. "Obviously, Kevin spilled his guts."

"Obviously." Dillon needed her to make a mistake, just a little one, so that he could get her gun off Sami. His own gun was a comforting bulk against his ankle, but did him little good until he had an edge. "I thought you were the poor victim in all this, Felicia."

"Do I look like a victim?" She laughed. "After tonight, I run the operation."

After tonight, she'd be in jail. He'd see to it.

"Let's go," Felicia said, nodding toward the door. She gestured with the light. "The guy who thinks he's the boss is waiting."

"My father?" Sami whispered in dismay.

Ricardo stopped short and looked at her. He glanced at Felicia, who laughed wholeheartedly, leaving Dillon to worry what the joke was. He had a grim feeling they weren't going to like it.

All he could do was hope Kevin came through as planned. "You're pretty tough now that you have a gun to hide behind," he said conversationally to Ricardo, hoping to stir up a fight. Anything to distract Felicia long enough so he could pull his gun.

Ricardo's face darkened. "You're not in a position to tick me off, Kinley."

It was true. And the way Felicia handled that gun made his heart lurch.

"We gave you a job when no one else would hire you," Sami said to Felicia. "We kept you, even when you were lazy."

"Why do you think that was, Sami? You'll have to ask your father."

Sami paled. She turned on Ricardo. "You don't have to go through with it," she said urgently. "You have more integrity than this, Ricardo. I know it. I've seen it."

Ricardo closed his eyes. Dillon bent to make his move, but stopped cold when he heard the unmistakable click as Felicia cocked her gun.

"How dare you do that to him," Felicia said icily to Sami. "You can't possibly understand. We were cheated, lied to."

"That's not our fault," Sami urged. "We can help."

Felicia shook her head. "Only revenge will help. Ricardo, search our friend here, down by his left foot." She smiled grimly when Ricardo straightened with Dillon's gun in his hand. "Let's go. Now."

Ricardo pushed Dillon toward the door, his own gun at his back. Sami followed with Felicia behind her.

Their only hope now was Kevin. Silently they walked down the hall, back out onto the airstrip, and into hangar one. At the lobby, Ricardo pushed Dillon in and moved aside. When Sami stepped over the threshold and paused, Felicia shoved her hard. She went down.

Ricardo yelled at Felicia while Dillon dropped to

Sami's side. He helped her to the couch, wincing at his sore ribs. He cupped her face and mouthed the words, *I love you*, swallowing hard at the returning emotion he saw so clearly. He pulled her dress together. Then caught his breath at the sight of her foot.

A two-inch-long gash bled profusely. Biting down on his rage, he looked at Ricardo. "I need a rag to stop the bleeding. She's cut badly, probably needs stitches."

Ricardo's mouth tightened, but Felicia only laughed. "Why bother? We're still going to dump them off in the Mexican desert on the next flight. A little cut isn't going to matter."

Ricardo's eyes stayed on Sami's blood-covered foot. "I *never* agreed to kill her."

Good, Dillon thought, *fight*. He needed the distraction. But first he had to staunch Sami's bleeding. Carefully he eased her torn stocking back from her foot. The cut flapped open, gushing blood. She definitely needed stitches, but he looked up into Sami's wide, pain-filled eyes and forced a smile. She didn't buy it.

"I won't kill her," Ricardo said adamantly.

"You won't have to. She'll die in the desert."

Sami sat up and said over Dillon's shoulder, "You don't have to do this, Ricardo. It's not too late to stop."

Felicia frowned and waved the gun at her. "Shut up, just shut up. Don't listen, Ricardo. Remember how we felt when Kevin betrayed us. He could have been one of us."

"He didn't have it in him to be like you," Dillon interjected, whipping off his shirt. He put it to Sami's cut and pressed hard, wincing when she cringed at the pressure. "Kevin is honest."

"Good thing too," Kevin quipped lightly from the

doorway. "Or I'd have ended up as ugly on the inside as she is on the outside." He stepped aside, revealing Clark prodding him along with a gun.

Felicia frowned. "You're early."

Clark shrugged and shoved Kevin down on the couch opposite him, where the brothers exchanged bleak looks.

"Clark," Sami said in disgust, "I should have known you'd show up sooner or later."

"You should have been nicer to me, Sami. You didn't have to get involved, you know. I only wanted the run of the place while your father was away."

"It's true, Sami," Ricardo said, his eyes sad. "I tried to keep you safe."

"He wasn't good enough for you, was he, Sami?" Felicia asked softly, watching with a glow of satisfaction as Ricardo's fists balled. "Let's go."

"We'll go when I say," Clark said, giving Felicia a look. "You're out of line here tonight. We'll discuss it later."

"No, we won't." Felicia smiled and shot him. As Clark crumpled to the ground, she laughed. "Ricardo, let's move it."

Ricardo didn't move but just kept staring at Sami, who was shaking and staring at Clark in shock.

Dillon's heart moved into his throat watching Ricardo watch Sami. The man's eyes ran over her torn dress as Sami uneasily yanked it back over her shoulder.

"Ricardo," Felicia said again. "Let's go."

"Five minutes," Ricardo said softly, moving toward Sami, who shrank back against Dillon.

"No," she whispered. "Ricardo, no."

Dillon wrapped his arms around Sami and eyed Ricardo. "Touch her and you're dead."

"Move away from her, Kinley," Ricardo warned. "I won't hurt her."

Years later, Dillon would still break out in a cold sweat thinking about this moment, but for now all he could do was watch in suspended disbelief as Kevin casually stuck out his foot and sent Ricardo sprawling.

Dillon leaped up and jumped on Ricardo, smashing his fist into the man's jaw. Yanking the gun from Clark's limp hand, he whirled in time to see Kevin running toward Felicia.

Sami screamed and flew at Dillon with such dizzying speed it was all he could do to grab her as they both started to fall.

A shot rang out, and he felt a slice of hot, sickening pain sheer through him, just as he remembered one very important thing.

Felicia had a gun.

FIFTEEN

Sami fell to the ground. She looked down and saw Dillon laying beneath her, eyes closed, face ashen. Blood pumped out of a small hole in his chest.

Everything switched to slow motion. She watched Felicia move her arm until her gun was trained on Kevin. Only she never fired. Instead she, too, crumpled to the ground in a doll-like fashion.

Standing behind her, holding an umbrella, was Howard Reed.

But Sami couldn't soak up that information, not when Dillon's blood flowed freely down his body and across her as she knelt beside him. Kevin flew to her side, pushed her out of the way as he ripped off his own shirt and pressed it hard to Dillon's shoulder. "Call the paramedics," he said tersely. "The police too." He didn't take his eyes off his brother.

Sami heard him swear, then felt him shake her hard. "Sami, please. Baby, come on. Snap out of it. I need you. Call the paramedics." She looked down where his hands had made bloody prints on her dress. Dillon's blood, she thought. She ran to the phone, wondering why her father didn't stop her. She made the call and dropped down beside a deathly still Dillon.

"I was too slow. Too damned slow." Kevin's face was grim. "Towels," he demanded as blood soaked through the shirt he'd placed against the wound. "Get me some towels."

The pain in her foot ceased to exist as she grabbed as many as she could find. She watched as Kevin worked to staunch the flow of blood, unmindful of her father holding vigil, with the gun and lethal umbrella on Felicia and the still-unconscious Clark and Ricardo.

Dillon moaned and tried to move. More blood flowed with his efforts to get up. "Dillon," she said in the calmest voice she could. "Please, lie still."

His eyes flashed open. "She . . . got me," he whispered in surprise.

"Yes," Sami whispered back, fighting her terrified tears. "But you're too tough to let her win."

Kevin pushed harder, and Dillon flinched. "I forgot how much a bullet hurt."

Her heart twisted, and she met Kevin's agonized gaze. "The paramedics are coming," she promised. He was in so much pain, it hurt to watch. She loved him. And she'd waited far too long to tell him. "Dillon—"

"Promise you'll show them your foot," he said, struggling to open his eyes. He reached for her and she grabbed his hands to keep them out of Kevin's way as he tried his best to slow the bleeding.

"Dillon," Kevin said, his voice wavering slightly. "Lie still, bud. You're bleeding all over the new carpet."

"Oh, there's gratitude for you . . . ," he trailed off with a groan when Kevin shifted the towels.

"Oh, please," Sami begged him. "Stop talking." She touched his face softly. He'd lost so much blood. "Dillon." She bent closer. "I love you." He didn't move. "Dillon?" She glanced at Kevin when he didn't respond. He reached to check Dillon's pulse.

"He's unconscious. Dammit! Where are the paramedics?"

Sami felt the tears build again. "He's lost so much blood." Kevin didn't say anything, but the look on his face did nothing to ease the hard knot of fear in her stomach.

"Samantha?" She glanced in surprise. Howard had a grip on his chest, his face a sickly gray. "I think you'd better come over here and take this gun." His face spasmed in pain. Sami ran to him, and he forced the gun into her palm. "Don't . . . don't let them hurt you," he said, slumping to the ground.

Sami turned in surprise to Felicia, and for the first time, the situation sank in. Her father had saved their lives. But why? Clark still hadn't moved. He could be dead. Felicia shifted and groaned. Sami nervously leveled the gun in her direction. "Tell me what's going on, Felicia."

"Surely you're not that stupid," she snapped, rubbing the back of her head. "I'd never work for your father."

"Was he in this or not?" Sami demanded, feeling the gun slip in her sweaty hands.

"Your father," she said bitterly, "couldn't handle it. Clark had to convince him."

"You mean blackmail," Kevin called out angrily.

A siren wailed in the distance, coming closer and louder.

"Sami," her father whispered. "I'm sorry. I called you last night. I wanted you safe and far away."

"How did they do it, Dad?" she asked him, holding his hands. "How did they blackmail you?"

He smiled sadly. "With you. They threatened you."

The police burst in, followed by the paramedics. Howard and Clark were whisked away on stretchers. An officer disarmed Sami, and she limped to Dillon's side as they loaded him too. "I want to ride with him."

One of the paramedics shook his head at Kevin, who swallowed hard and squeezed Sami close, restraining her. "I'll drive you."

She clung to him, not sure who comforted whom, as the police started in on their questions. Sami could pay attention to none of it, her head felt so light. She jerked in surprise as Kevin picked her up and carried her out the front door of the lobby.

"I'm taking you to the hospital," he said firmly. "The police are done here."

She glanced in confusion as she saw Ricardo and Felicia being led out. "Dillon."

Kevin's jaw tightened. "We'll go to him. Soon as they look at you." He put her in Dillon's Jeep.

"He's not going to die, Kevin." She squeezed his hands and fought tears. "He can't. He didn't hear me tell him I love him."

His eyes suspiciously bright, he gave her a quick, hard hug. "He knows, Sami. He knows. And he won't die. He's too stubborn."

His voice seemed so wobbly, so unreassuring, that Sami wanted to cry. "He lost so much blood."

"Well, I'll go give him more." He gave her a tight smile. "He'll be all right. He has to be. He's all I have left."

Kevin paced the waiting-room floor at the hospital for the thousandth time, and from where Sami sat in her chair, her eyes burning with unshed tears, she smiled sadly. With his long legs, broad shoulders, and tense, rugged features, he looked very much like his older brother. She couldn't imagine how she hadn't noticed before.

"Kevin, come rest. We've been up all night. You've got to be exhausted."

"The surgery should have been over by now," he said restlessly, coming to a stop near Sami. "Clark's was over hours ago. I can't believe that bastard's going to live. Why can't they tell us about Dillon?" His agonized green eyes stared down at her.

"They will." She rubbed at her eyes wearily. "You're the one who should be resting. Go get some sleep in that bed they gave you. I'll come get you when there's news."

"No," she said firmly. "I'm not leaving."

"Oh, my God." Lucy stood in the doorway, pale and shaken.

"Lucy." Both Kevin and Sami spoke her name at once. Sami's tired eyes filled yet again at the tenderness in Kevin's gaze as he looked at her friend.

"I don't believe it," Lucy whispered, staring at Kevin, though her eyes held excitement and hope. "It's really you . . . isn't it?"

He moved toward her, smiling. "It's me." He wiped

a tear from her face with his fingers and whispered, "I'm back."

She gave a little laugh. "But . . . how?"

"It's complicated," he admitted. "But I'm glad you're here."

Lucy wrapped her arms around him. "I've dreamed of this."

"Me too." His voice was hoarse, and his arms closed around her. "Me too."

Sami's head ached with emotion at the bittersweet and poignant moment. "I don't understand any of this," Lucy said. "But I heard about Dillon. How is he?"

"We don't know yet—" She broke off as the surgeon came into the waiting room with a tired smile.

"He's out of surgery. The bullet's been removed." Sami sagged in relief until his next words. "It hit a major artery and he took six pints of blood. He'll be one sore man for a while, but it's doubtful there'll be permanent damage."

Kevin came close and took her hand, looking haggard. "Six pints of blood . . . he nearly bled to death."

"Yes," the surgeon agreed solemnly. "He's in recovery." He looked at Sami. "He's calling for you. You'll want to see him."

More than anything.

Sami smiled when Dillon opened his eyes and blinked her into focus. She wanted to throw herself across his chest and sob out the horror of the last couple of days, but he looked so awful, she forced herself to be strong.

When he reached for her hand, she lost it. She loved him so very much, and she'd come so very close to losing him. There wasn't an ounce of strength left in her. She bent her head on his chest and cried, her body racked with her pent-up emotions. Even being mortified over her lack of control couldn't stop the flow.

"Sami?" Dillon patted her back, and she cried harder. "Sami, come on, look at me."

She couldn't. Then she heard his frustrated curse and felt him try to shift. "No," she said with a gasp, sniffling and lifting her head. "Don't move."

"Then come here. No, on my bed." She sat on the edge. "Are you okay?" he asked, his gaze searching her face.

She nodded, and when he lifted a hand to wipe her tears, she turned her face into his palm and kissed it.

"Kevin?"

"He's fine too," she assured him with a watery smile.

"Your foot?"

"Dillon," she said with a hopeless laugh that was filled with all the love in her heart. "We're all fine." He looked pale, sweaty, and as if he needed pain medication. "I'm getting the nurse."

"Not yet." He gripped her hand with amazing strength. "Did they look at your foot?"

"You're impossible." She sniffed again. "Yes, if you must know. Eight stitches. And it hurt."

He winced. "I'm sorry. I wanted to be there."

"Please, I'm fine. You've got to worry about yourself." She could tell she would have to annoy him into it. "Besides," she added with a little smile. "Your brother held my hand."

"Figures." He gave a look of mock disgust as Kevin came into the room. "He always did try to steal my girl."

His girl. The corny words warmed her heart.

"I did not," Kevin protested with a grin.

"Did too." He closed his eyes. "He can't get his own, you know."

"That just goes to show you what you know. Lucy might say otherwise."

"Really?" Dillon asked, his lips curving.

"Really." Kevin leaned against the bed and looked down worriedly, his smile fading. "You scared us to death, Dillon. Don't do that again, man. My ticker can't take it." He pressed a hand to his heart.

"Speaking of that," Dillon said, stroking Sami's hand. "How's your father?"

"Back in the hospital. But alive."

"And?" he prodded, watching her.

She sighed. "And thinking it's pretty amusing that you thought he was the bad guy when he thought you were."

Dillon's lips curved again. "I guess I owe the man." He squeezed her hand. "On two accounts."

"Dillon," she whispered with a self-conscious glance at Kevin. She had to tell him.

Kevin took his cue gallantly and gave them a roguish smile tinged with the energy of a high-powered relief. "I'm going." He headed toward the door, whistling lightly. Sami leaned over Dillon to look at his bandages.

He gripped her shoulders. "Do you love me, Sami?"

She sucked in her breath at the blunt question,

taken off guard. The enormity of her feelings for him scared her beyond belief.

"Do you?"

"Yes," she admitted miserably. "Yes."

Something flickered in his light eyes. Relief. "Then tell me, dammit."

"I . . . love you." She slumped. "Whew."

"Hard, huh?" He tsked sympathetically, but ruined it with a grin. "It's not a death sentence."

"It's scary."

His warm, beautiful smile melted her heart. "But fun."

"More like one of those roller-coaster rides your friends make you get on that won't stop." She felt sick.

He laughed, then swallowed hard with a grimace. With a lightning speed that belied his supposed pain and weakness, he snagged her hips and nudged her so that she lay across him. She braced herself up off his chest and shoulder with her arms, gasping in dismay. "Don't! Are you in much pain?"

"Yes. It aches right here." He pushed his hips up against hers, grinning at her shocked expression when she came in contact with his "ache."

"You're crazy." She tried to push herself upright, panicked she'd hurt him.

Plowing his fingers into her hair, he took her mouth in a kiss that left her shaky and breathless. "I've waited so long," he whispered against her lips. "So long for you to tell me you loved me. You've tortured me on purpose, haven't you?" But before she could answer, he'd claimed her lips again until she swam in the powerful feelings he evoked. She loved him so much it hurt.

"Look at me, Sami."

She lifted her gaze and saw only blinding love. For her. His voice came low, urgent, all traces of merriment and lust gone. "I love you. I want to spend the rest of my life with you." He gave her one of his irresistible, cajoling smiles. "Come on, Sami. Say you feel the same, because I don't think I can let you go."

"What if I don't?" she asked him seriously, though her heart thrilled to his words and a mixture of laughter and tears filled her eyes.

"You need me," he said, shifting tactics with the ease of a man who could talk himself out of—and into—anything. "Think of how many times I've had to save you."

She raised her eyebrows. "I saved you too."

"Whatever." He shrugged, obviously unwilling to be bothered with minute details. His eyes pierced hers. "Too chicken?"

"I'm not."

He looked at her for a long time. "I think you are," he said gently.

She gave up gracefully and lay on his good side, burying her face in his neck. "What if you change your mind?"

He shook his head in bewilderment and pushed her back up so he could see her face. "Sami, wouldn't you call me, well, stubborn?"

She laughed. "Yeah. Kinda."

"Look up the meaning sometime. I say what I mean and I stick with it." He tugged a lock of her hair. "I'm going to always love you, Sami. Forever."

She felt her mouth fall open. "You mean . . . you want to marry me?"

He gave a short laugh. "Yeah," he said. "I want to marry you. Okay?"

She stared at him in wonder. "Okay," she whispered. The fear deserted her, leaving a delicious warm, fuzzy feeling. "Okay," she said again on a laugh. "I love you, Dillon."

"See? That didn't hurt a bit this time. Did it?"

"No." She grinned. "I love you. I love you. I love you."

His grin spread. "Now that that's taken care of . . ." He twisted his hips again, reminding her of his problem. "Do something for my pain."

She smiled wickedly. "Oh, I can fix that," she assured him with a hot, wet kiss.

THE EDITORS' CORNER

Happy anniversary! No, not you—us! June 1997 marks the fourteenth anniversary of LOVESWEPT. Many of you have been with us since the inception of LOVESWEPT. For that, we thank you and we hope to continue our strong relationship with our loyal readers. Speaking of relationships, have we got some doozies for you! Our fourteenth anniversary lineup includes everything from corporate intrigue, pretend weddings, diamonds, and babies. (And not necessarily in that order!) Oh yeah, remember last month's editors' corner where we told you to keep an eye out for that "new, yet traditional look" in LOVESWEPT's future? Well, the future is now, baby!

With his company at stake as well as his heart, Rio Thornton must guard himself from the golden-eyed corporate princess Yasmine Damaron in **THE DAMARON MARK: THE HEIRESS,** LOVE-

SWEPT #838, by bestselling author Fayrene Preston. A trademark Damaron, Yasmine is very much in control of herself and her heart, but when she faces the fiercely masculine executive, the heat of his desire stuns and arouses her. She makes Rio an offer he can't refuse, insisting that she's only after his business, but Rio's heart is the soul of his business. Can he give his heart away without losing the one thing he needs most? With a story that's both sensual and charming, Fayrene Preston is back, in this latest installment of the Damaron series.

In Destiny, Texas, there is a force at work: a fortune-teller with mystical powers of foresight. However, in Karen Leabo's **BRIDES OF DESTINY: MILLICENT'S MEDICINE MAN,** LOVE-SWEPT #839, Millicent Whitney, a widow and expectant mother, refuses to believe that Dr. Jase Desmond is the one for her. She's already had the love of her life and now he's dead, leaving her with a baby on the way. Way out of his league, neurosurgeon Jase Desmond helps to deliver Millicent's baby and realizes that he's been denying himself for far too long. Can Jase teach Millicent that loving again isn't betraying a memory but opening her heart to new dreams? In this poignant love story of new beginnings and second chances, Karen Leabo explores the funny and tender side of starting over, with this last chapter of the Brides of Destiny series.

Suzanne Brockmann returns with another sexy and charming comedy in **STAND-IN GROOM,** LOVESWEPT #840. Chelsea Spencer has to get married in order to receive her inheritance, but the man she's chosen has just RSVPed his regrets. Suddenly she remembers the handsome (and interested) stranger who'd saved her from being mugged. When she offers Johnny Anziano the opportunity to make his dreams come true, Johnny jumps at the chance to get to know Chelsea, even if it includes marrying her first. Chelsea and Johnny's shaky alliance means a risky marital charade and a spirited romp that is irresistibly seductive and utterly romantic.

Fate. Faith. The laws of divine reciprocity. Drake Tallen has his own word to define the priceless gem he found: Justice. In **FLAWLESS**, LOVESWEPT #841, Drake knows that this perfect gem will lure Emery Brooks back home long enough for him to exact his sweet revenge on his almost-bride-to-be. Ten years ago, Emery had run from the small Indiana town to an empty life in Chicago. Now tasked with buying the gem from Drake, Emery must face the man she loved and left, but can she resist his dark desire and the memories too strong to deny? And can she do it without surrendering her heart for the perfect stone? Cynthia Powell's latest novel delivers one surprise after another in a story sizzling with sensual secrets.

Happy reading!

With warmest wishes,

Shauna Summers

Joy Abella

Shauna Summers
Editor

Joy Abella
Administrative Editor

P.S. Look for these Bantam women's fiction titles coming in June. *New York Times* bestselling author Amanda Quick stuns the romance world with **AF-FAIR**. Private investigator Charlotte Arkendale doesn't know what to make of Baxter St. Ives, her new man-of-affairs. He claims to be a respectable gentleman, but something in his eyes proclaims otherwise. Fellow *New York Times* bestselling author Nora Roberts delivers **SWEET REVENGE**, now available again in paperback. Just as Princess Adrianne is poised to taste the sweetness of her long-awaited vengeance, she finds herself up against two formidable men—one with the knowledge to take her freedom, the other with the power to take her life. In the tradition of PRINCE OF SHADOWS and PRINCE OF WOLVES, Susan Krinard returns with **TWICE A HERO**. Adventurer Mac Sinclair is fascinated by the exploits of her grandfather and his partner Liam O'Shea. When she becomes disoriented inside the ruins in the Mayan jungles, she bumps into Liam O'Shea himself . . . alive, well, and seductively real—in the year 1884! Historical romance favorite Adrienne deWolfe puts the finishing touch on her Texas trilogy with **TEXAS WILDCAT**, a story about a man and a woman who are on opposite sides of the fence. As Bailey McShane and Zach Rawlins struggle with the drought that's tearing the state apart, they slowly realize that being together is the thing that matters most.

Don't miss these extraordinary books
by your favorite Bantam authors!

On sale in April:

MISCHIEF
by Amanda Quick

ONCE A WARRIOR
by Karyn Monk

Now available in paperback

MISCHIEF

by *New York Times* bestselling author

Amanda Quick

*To help her foil a ruthless fortune hunter, Imogen
Waterstone needs a man.
Not just any man, but Matthias Marshall,
the intrepid explorer known as
"Cold-blooded Colchester."*

"You pass yourself off as a man of action, but
now it seems that you are not that sort of man at
all," Imogen told Matthias.

"I do not pass myself off as anything but what
I am, you exasperating little—"

"Apparently you write fiction rather than fact,
sir. Bad enough that I thought you to be a clever,
resourceful gentleman given to feats of daring. I
have also been laboring under the equally mis-
taken assumption that you are a man who would
put matters of honor ahead of petty consider-
ations of inconvenience."

"Are you calling my honor as well as my man-
hood into question?"

"Why shouldn't I? You are clearly indebted to

me, sir, yet you obviously wish to avoid making payment on that debt."

"I was indebted to your uncle, not to you."

"I have explained to you that I inherited the debt," she retorted.

Matthias took another gliding step into the grim chamber. "Miss Waterstone, you try my patience."

"I would not dream of doing so," she said, her voice dangerously sweet. "I have concluded that you will not do at all as an associate in my scheme. I hereby release you from your promise. Begone, sir."

"Bloody hell, woman. You are not going to get rid of me so easily." Matthias crossed the remaining distance between them with two long strides and clamped his hands around her shoulders.

Touching her was a mistake. Anger metamorphosed into desire in the wink of an eye.

For an instant he could not move. His insides seemed to have been seized by a powerful fist. Matthias tried to breathe, but Imogen's scent filled his head, clouding his brain. He looked down into the bottomless depths of her blue-green eyes and wondered if he would drown. He opened his mouth to conclude the argument with a suitably repressive remark, but the words died in his throat.

The outrage vanished from Imogen's gaze. It was replaced by sudden concern. "My lord? Is something wrong?"

"Yes." It was all he could do to get the word past his teeth.

"What is it?" She began to look alarmed. "Are you ill?"

"Quite possibly."

"Good heavens. I had not realized. That no doubt explains your odd behavior."

"No doubt."

"Would you care to lie down on the bed for a few minutes?"

"I do not think that would be a wise move at this juncture." She was so soft. He could feel the warmth of her skin through the sleeves of her prim, practical gown. He realized that he longed to discover if she made love with the same impassioned spirit she displayed in an argument. He forced himself to remove his hands from her shoulders. "We had best finish this discussion at some other time."

"Nonsense," she said bracingly. "I do not believe in putting matters off, my lord."

Matthias shut his eyes for the space of two or three seconds and took a deep breath. When he lifted his lashes he saw that Imogen was watching him with a fascinated expression. "Miss Waterstone," he began with grim determination. "I am trying to employ reason here."

"You're going to help me, aren't you?" She started to smile.

"I beg your pardon?"

"You've changed your mind, haven't you? Your sense of honor has won out." Her eyes glowed. "Thank you, my lord. I knew you would assist me in my plans." She gave him an approving little pat on the arm. "And you must not concern yourself with the other matter."

"What other matter?"

"Why, your lack of direct experience with bold feats and daring adventure. I quite understand. You need not be embarrassed by the fact that you are not a man of action, sir."

"Miss Waterstone—"

"Not everyone can be an intrepid sort, after all," she continued blithely. "You need have no fear. If anything dangerous occurs in the course of my scheme, I shall deal with it."

"The very thought of you taking charge of a dangerous situation is enough to freeze the marrow in my bones."

"Obviously you suffer from a certain weakness of the nerves. But we shall contrive to muddle through. Try not to succumb to the terrors of the imagination, my lord. I know you must be extremely anxious about what lies ahead, but I assure you, I will be at your side every step of the way."

"Will you, indeed?" He felt dazed.

"I shall protect you." Without any warning, Imogen put her arms around him and gave him what was no doubt meant to be a quick, reassuring hug.

The tattered leash Matthias was using to hold on to his self-control snapped. Before Imogen could pull away, he wrapped her close.

"Sir?" Her eyes widened with surprise.

"The only aspect of this situation that truly alarms me, Miss Waterstone," he said roughly, "is the question of who will protect me from you?"

Her stories are tender and sensual,
humorous and deeply involving. Now
Karyn Monk offers her most enthralling
romance ever . . . a tale of a shattered
hero fighting for redemption—and fighting
for love. . . .

ONCE A
WARRIOR

Karyn Monk

"Karyn Monk . . . brings the romance of the
era to readers with her spellbinding storytelling
talents. This is a new author to watch."
—*Romantic Times*

*Ariella MacKendrick knew her people had only one
hope for survival: she must find the mighty warrior
known as the Black Wolf and bring him home to
defend her clan. But when Ariella finally tracks him
down, Malcolm MacFane is nothing like the hero she
dreamed he would be. The fearless laird who once led
a thousand men is a drunken shell of his former self,
scarred inside and out, with no army in sight. Yet
Ariella has no choice but to put her trust in MacFane.*

And soon something begins to stir in the fallen legend. A fire still rages in his warrior heart—a passion that could lead them into battle . . . a desire, barely leashed, that could brand a Highland beauty's soul.

"Turn onto your stomach, MacFane," she instructed quietly.

He did not argue but simply did as she told him. Ariella suspected the powder she had given him had taken effect.

Now that he was on his front, it was far easier for her to massage him. She focused on the valley of his back for a while, and when she was finished, she placed one of the warm swine bladders on it, so the muscles could absorb the heat. Then she moved up, gently kneading the solid layers of spasm on each side of his spine. Little by little the hardness beneath her fingers began to yield. Her touch grew firmer, delved deeper, encouraging the muscles to release their grip. When her hands began to ache, she retrieved the other swine bladder, which she had kept warm before the fire, and gently placed it on his upper back.

MacFane's eyes were closed and he was breathing deeply, his head resting against his arm. Wanting him to be as comfortable as possible, Ariella removed his boots, examining his injured leg as she did so. He had told her it was shattered when his horse collapsed on it. She ran her hands up the muscled calf, bent it slightly at the knee, then continued her journey along his thigh. The bone seemed straight enough, and from what she could tell he had not lost any length. But she knew a bad break could plague a person with pain for the rest of his life. The leg was stiff, so she rubbed some ointment into her palms and began to massage it. After watching him limp this past month, she wondered if there was anything that could be done to ease the ache and strengthen the muscles. Perhaps with exercise—

"I didn't fall."

She looked up at him, surprised that he was still awake. "Pardon?"

"I didn't fall," he repeated thickly. "Someone put a spur under my saddle."

"I know." She continued to massage his leg.

He nodded with satisfaction and closed his eyes again. "I'm not in the habit of falling off my goddamn horse." The words were slurred, but she could hear the anger in them.

She thought of him thundering into her camp wielding his sword in both hands. No, MacFane was not in the habit of falling off his horse. Someone was trying to drive him away. The arrow hadn't worked, so they put a spur under his saddle, knowing the fall would not only injure him physically but would humiliate him in front of the entire clan.

"I think it was Niall," he mumbled.

She paused. "Why do you say that?"

"He has never tried to hide his contempt for me." He lifted his lids and regarded her a moment, his blue eyes suddenly intense. "And I've seen the way he looks at you." His expression was dark, as if the matter angered him. Then he sighed and closed his eyes once more.

Ariella considered this. Niall had shared her loathing toward MacFane when he failed to answer her father's missive. She had even encouraged his fury when her clan was attacked and MacFane never came. But while she could understand his expressing his contempt, could Niall actually be trying to drive him away? To do so would not be in the best interest of the clan. Was it possible his rage was that great?

Deeply disturbed by the possibility, she removed the cooling swine bladders from MacFane's back. He shifted onto his side, his head still resting on the hard pillow of his arm, his dark brown hair spilling loosely over his massive shoulder. Deciding she would bind his ribs with the linen strips tomorrow, she drew a blanket over him, then stayed there a moment, studying him.

He exuded an extraordinary aura of power and vulnerability as he lay there, injured and drugged, yet somehow still formidable. How cruelly ironic, that after fighting so many battles as the great Black Wolf, his greatest enemy now was his own body. Perhaps she had asked too much of him by bringing him here to train her people. From early morning to late evening he labored, training, planning, overseeing the fortifications to the castle. His demanding days would exhaust a man at the peak of his physical abilities, never mind one for whom it was an effort to cross a room or mount the stairs. And now someone was determined to force him from here, even if it meant injuring him in the process. It was wrong to expect he should remain under such circumstances, even if he had promised to remain until they found a new laird. She must send him away as soon as he was fit to ride, before he was even more injured than he had been today. In his current state he could do nothing more to help them. It was now up to her to find a warrior with an army who could wield the sword.

Yet as she stood beside him watching the even rise and fall of his chest, she could not help but wonder what would happen to MacFane when he left. He had no family or clan who would joyously celebrate his return. Instead he would go back to the dank, filthy hut he shared with Gavin, where his days would be nothing but long, empty hours filled with pain, drink, and bitterness. While this fact had never bothered her before, suddenly she found the idea abhorrent. However MacFane had failed his people, did he really deserve to be condemned to such a miserable existence?

His brow was creased, indicating he still struggled with his pain. He moaned slightly and buried his face in his arm, as if trying to escape his discomfort. A dark lock of hair slipped across the clenched line of his jaw. Without thinking, Ariella leaned over and gently brushed the hair off his face, her fingers grazing the sandy surface of his cheek. MacFane's hand instantly clamped around her wrist, binding her to him with bruising force.

He opened his eyes and glared at her, his gaze menacing as he fought to clear the mists of alcohol and herbs. When he realized who she was, his grip eased, but he did not release her. Instead he pulled her down, until she hovered barely a breath away from him.

"I will not leave you, Ariella," he whispered roughly, "until I know you are safe."

Ariella stared at him, her heart beating rapidly, wondering how he could have known what she was thinking. "You cannot stay, MacFane," she countered. "Whoever wants you gone will not stop until you are dead."

Malcolm released her wrist and waited for her to move away from him. When she did not, he hesitantly laid his fingers against her cheek. "I'm already dead," he murmured, fascinated by the softness of her skin. "I have been for a long time."

They stayed like that a moment, staring at each other. And then, overcome with weariness, Malcolm sighed and drifted into sleep, his hand still pressed against the silk of Ariella's cheek.

On sale in May:

AFFAIR
by *Amanda Quick*

TWICE A HERO
by *Susan Krinard*

TEXAS WILDCAT
by *Adrienne deWolfe*